BUBBLEMANIA
A CHEWY HISTORY OF BUBBLE GUM

By Lee Wardlaw

Illustrated by Sandra Forrest

Aladdin Paperbacks

25 Years of Magical Reading

ALADDIN PAPERBACKS
EST. 1972

First Aladdin Paperbacks edition September 1997

Aladdin Paperbacks
An imprint of Simon & Schuster
Children's Publishing Division
1230 Avenue of the Americas
New York, NY 10020

Designed by Sandra Forrest

The text of this book was set in Garamond.
Printed and bound in the United States of America

10 9 8 7 6 5 4 3 2 1

Library of Congress Cataloging-in-Publication Data

Wardlaw, Lee, 1955-
Bubblemania / Lee Wardlaw. —1st Aladdin Paperbacks ed.
p. cm.
Includes bibliographical references (p.).
Summary: Discusses bubble gum, including important people in the world of bubble gum, its invention and
history, how it is manufactured and sold today, and gives advice on how to blow really great bubbles.
ISBN 0-689-81719-3
1. Bubble gum—Juvenile literature. [1. Bubble gum. 2. Chewing gum.] I. Title.
TX799.W37 1997
641.3'3—dc21
97-2522
CIP
AC

PERMISSIONS

"For Better or Ill." Copyright 1993 by Julia Cunningham. Used with permission.
"Bodacious Billy the Bubble King." Copyright 1993 by Ellen A. Kelley. Used with permission.
"Sticky Limerick." Copyright 1993 by Lisa Merkl. Used with permission.
"Recipe for Bubble Gum." Copyright 1994 by Dian Curtis Regan. Used with permission.
"Basketball Can be a Thrill." Copyright 1991 by Topps, Inc. Used with permission.
Photos on the half-title and dedication pages: Courtesy John Wardlaw.

For Jessica and Russell McLoughlin,
who know it's wads of fun to get
stuck on reading!

BUBBLEMANIA
A CHEWY HISTORY OF BUBBLE GUM

ONCE UPON A CHEW

*"I just adore gum. I can't do without it.
I munch it all day long except for a few minutes
at mealtimes when I take it out and stick it
behind my ear for safekeeping."*

—Violet Beauregarde in
Charlie and the Chocolate Factory,
by Roald Dahl, 1964

Do you savor those first few chews of a new piece of bubble gum, when your mouth fills with that slurpy, syrupy sweetness?

Do you dig for pennies in your pocket whenever you pass a machine brimming with rainbow-colored gum balls?

Have you ever blown a bubble the size of a cantaloupe and had it explode all over your face?

Do you think Bazooka Joe might be a good name for your dog—even if it's a girl?

9

Humans are the only animals on earth that chew gum. Dental scientist Carl Kleber says, "You can get a monkey to chew it for a couple of minutes, but then they just take it out and stick it in their hair."

When your bubble gum loses its flavor, do you cram in another chunk? And another? And *another?*

Do you like to *thwack* your gum? Chomp your gum? Snap-crackle-and-pop your gum?

If you answered yes to any of these questions, then you're a bubble-maniac—a person who is *crazy* about bubble gum.

You're not alone. Millions of people have munched billions of wads since bubble gum first popped onto the scene in 1906. If you stuck together every piece that's ever been chewed, you'd have a stick 113 million miles long. That's long enough to reach the moon and back *two hundred times.*

Americans spend about $500 million a year on the chewy, gooey stuff. But gum-chewing isn't just an American phenomenon. Today, there are bubblemaniacs in more than one hundred countries around the world.

Some Eskimos now like chewing bubble gum better than whale blubber. Rumors tell of a certain African tribe that traded wives for bubble gum instead of the usual sheep and

oxen. In Borneo, a diplomat was kidnapped by headhunters who demanded a ransom of—you guessed it—bubble gum.

Why is bubble gum so popular? Who was the first to make it? How, when, and where did bubblemania get started?

The story begins . . . Once upon a chew. . . .

THE FLINTSTONES MEET CHEWING GUM

Psychologists believe the urge to chew is innate, which means we're born with it. As babies, we suckle for milk. As we grow older, we munch on food. But the urge to chew remains, even between meals. Why?

One explanation is that chewing relieves stress and anxiety. This is true whether you're a caveman preparing to battle a saber-toothed tiger or a sixth grader about to give an oral report.

Another explanation is that chewing nonedible objects kept our ancestors' teeth clean and strong. Stone Age cultures around the world gnawed on sticks, whale blubber, and animal gristle. Today, we keep our teeth and gums healthy with toothbrushes and dental floss. But you might still catch yourself nibbling on a pencil, rubber band, or a blade of grass on a hot summer afternoon.

For years, anthropologists suspected that Stone Age people also chewed resin, a gummy substance found in certain pine trees. They proved their theory in 1932, when the skeletons of a prehistoric family were discovered inside a cave in Texas. Pieces of ABC (Already-Been-Chewed) resin gum lay beside them!

Swedish archaeologists stumbled upon another primitive wad in 1993. Dark in color and sweetened with honey, the resin gum bears the teeth marks of a Stone Age teenager. The gum is nine thousand years old—the oldest ever found.

It's obvious that even our Flintstone-like ancestors enjoyed chomping gum as much as we do.

Yabba-dabba-chew!

It's Greek to Me

Zeus and Athena. Socrates and Aristotle. The Olympic Games and the Trojan horse. The ancient Greeks gave us great myths, great thinkers, great sports, and great tricks. They also gave us great gum.

The first written record of gum chewing dates back to the first century A.D. In his book *De Materia Medica,* the Greek doctor-botanist Dioscondes recommended the chewing of *mastiche* (pronounced mas-tee-ka) as a treatment for minor illnesses. *Mastiche* is a yellowish resin or sap taken from the bark of small evergreen trees. Women especially enjoyed chewing *mastiche,* or mastic gum, as a way to clean their teeth and sweeten their breath.

Many Greeks and Middle Easterners chew mastic gum today, although they now combine it with beeswax for a softer, easier chew.

Maya Borrow a Piece of Gum?

The Greeks weren't the only people in ancient times with a highly developed civilization. Over a thousand years ago, in the jungles of Central America, the Maya Indians built beautiful cities with towering temples and sophisticated highways. They created the most accurate calendar of their time and became brilliant astronomers and mathematicians.

They also enjoyed chewing gum.

One of the staples in the Mayan diet was the fruit from the sapodilla tree (now known as the chewing gum tree). While trying to harvest the fruit, someone may have accidentally cut the bark, causing a creamy juice called latex to ooze from the tree. When the latex came in contact with the air, it thickened into a gummy mass that the Maya called chicle. Centuries later, chicle would become the main ingredient in modern chewing gum.

As early as the year 200, the Maya were chewing chicle after meals to aid their digestion. They also used it as a refreshing pick-me-up, just as we do today when we're tired or bored. Although chicle has no flavor, the Maya liked its smooth, velvety texture. Because it quenched their thirst, they brought chicle on long journeys, tucking a wad into their mouth to keep their cheeks and tongue moist. They even wrapped rolls of it in banana leaves to create the first "packaged" gum.

The Maya often used chicle to make rubber shoes or galoshes. They did this by dipping their bare feet into the goo. The latex then thickened and hardened to the shape of their feet.

When Christopher Columbus reached Santo Domingo (now Dominican Republic) in 1492, he saw natives chewing mastic gum. He wrote about this custom in a letter to Lord Raphael Sanchez, one of the sponsors for his journey to the New World.

By the year 900, most Mayas had mysteriously abandoned their great cities. No one knows why they left or where they went. Only the ruins of a few pyramids remain, hidden in the tangled growth of the rain forest. Yet, some descendents of the original Maya civilization still live in the jungle—and still enjoy chewing chicle.

A worker climbs a "chewing gum tree" in the jungles of South America. Using a machete, he makes shallow, V-shaped cuts in the trunk to release the milky latex or sap.

FROM THE HALLS OF MONTEZUMA TO THE SHORES OF PLYMOUTH ROCK

Imagine it's the sixteenth century. You're a Spanish conquistador, ready for battle, sword at your side. You've just traveled thousands of miles with your soldiers to Mexico. You plan to overthrow the great Aztec emperor, Montezuma II, and loot his cities of gold.

You find plenty of gold, all right. But you also find . . . chewing gum?

Yes, if you're Hernando Cortés.

When Cortés conquered Mexico in 1520, he marveled at the Aztecs, whose teeth were the whitest he had ever seen. He credited their healthy smiles to the Indians' habit of chewing chicle—a habit the Aztecs had learned from their Mayan ancestors.

Cortés never traveled as far north as Plymouth Rock, Massachusetts. But if he had, he might have discovered another Indian people that liked to chew gum: the Wampanoags.

The tropical sapodilla tree that produced chicle could not grow in the harsh winter climate of New England. But more than thirty varieties of spruce trees did. For centuries, Native Americans had enjoyed the tangy flavor of spruce resin. They used it as a thirst quencher, as the Maya had done. When the Pilgrims and other settlers arrived in the early 1600s, the Wampanoags offered them samples of their prized resin. On that first Thanksgiving, you might have heard a Pilgrim say, "Please pass a drumstick—and a lump of gum!"

During the next two hundred years, chewing spruce resin became a popular pastime among New Englanders. Settlers learned from the Indians which trees produced the most

In Sweden, spruce gum (called kada) was thought to cure a variety of mild diseases. Kada became so valued that gentlemen often gave it to their sweethearts. The early loggers in New England also gave spruce resin to their children, friends, or sweethearts. Usually they would whittle a small, hollow barrel from a block of wood, then fill it with globs of fragrant gum.

gum (those exposed to sun, wind, and rain) and which produced the chewiest gum (a mixture of Maine's black and red spruces—favorites of the Kennebec Indians).

In the first half of the nineteenth century, loggers or lumberjacks worked hard to fill the market for spruce gum. Each logger needed to harvest sixty pounds of raw gum a day to keep up with the demand. Little did they know how that demand would grow. Soon, an innovative young man equipped with a Franklin stove, a pot full of resin, and a grand idea would become the world's first commercial chewing gum manufacturer.

When the bark of a spruce tree is cut, a warning system inside the tree causes resin to fill and seal the break. This is much like putting a bandage on a sore, to help a wound heal. These rock-hard "Band-Aids" are what loggers would chop off with an ax to make spruce chewing gum.

CHAPTER
2

LUMBERJACKS AND FRANKLIN STOVES: JOHN B. CURTIS

> *"Do you love rats?" [asked Tom Sawyer of Becky Thatcher]*
> *"No! I hate them!"*
> *"Well, I do, too—live ones. But I mean dead ones, to swing round your head with a string."*
> *"No, I don't care for rats much, anyway. What I like is chewing gum."*
> *"Oh, I should say so. I wish I had some now."*
> *"Do you? I've got some. I'll let you chew it a while, but you must give it back to me."*
> *That was agreeable, so they chewed it turn about, and dangled their legs against a bench in excess of contentment.*
> —from *The Adventures of Tom Sawyer*, by Mark Twain, 1876

n Missouri in the 1840s, Becky Thatcher shared her nugget of Already-Been-Chewed gum with her secret love Tom Sawyer. At the same time, a young man from Bangor,

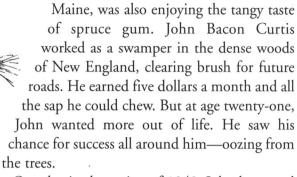

Maine, was also enjoying the tangy taste of spruce gum. John Bacon Curtis worked as a swamper in the dense woods of New England, clearing brush for future roads. He earned five dollars a month and all the sap he could chew. But at age twenty-one, John wanted more out of life. He saw his chance for success all around him—oozing from the trees.

One day in the spring of 1848, John harvested a few hunks of spruce resin and took them home to his parents. He said he had a plan to sell the gum commercially. First, they would need to boil the raw gum to thicken and purify it. Then they would cut and package it. Then they would have to convince local merchants to stock and sell it in their stores.

The elder Mr. Curtis had doubts. Who would buy a packaged gum from a store when you could buy it fresh-cut from a logger? But John argued and coaxed, and finally, his father agreed to help. They would start a company called Curtis and Son. John's father would produce the gum. John would be responsible for sales.

That afternoon, in a large kettle on his mother's Franklin stove, John cooked up his first batch of State of Maine Pure Spruce Gum.

DRUMMING UP BUSINESS

"Give a man all you can for his money, while making a fair profit for yourself." That became John's motto. He priced his new product at two "chaws" for a penny, and set out on foot to market the gum to the stores of Portland, Maine.

Two whole days later, an exhausted John finally found a shopkeeper willing to carry the gum. It sold out right away. Gradually, other stores agreed to stock it. But on the whole, sales were too slow to keep Curtis and Son in business for very long. So John made a decision: He would take State of Maine Pure Spruce Gum on the road.

For the next two years, John trekked through New England, peddling his gum from sunup to well past sundown. "I was on the road while the other fellow was in bed," John boasted. Some historians believe he was one of the country's first drummers, or traveling salesmen. And sell he did, traveling by horse cart, stagecoach, canal boat, steamboat, and sometimes by foot.

"I passed hundreds of nights camping out with only a blanket for a covering and the ground for a bed," John later reminisced. "[I] did object to the rattlesnakes sometimes. It didn't pay to have them get too familiar. . . ."

But the hard work did pay—and paid well. Curtis and Son earned five thousand dollars their first year in business. (A small amount by today's standards, but remember, John previously had earned five dollars a month as a swamper, which meant an income of only *sixty dollars a year.*)

Thousands of new customers tried the gum, and then bought more. And more. Father and son could hardly keep up with the demand. After a while they stopped harvesting the resin themselves. Instead, they bought gum from lumberjacks, trappers, farmers, and "gummers"—woodsmen who gathered spruce resin in March, the peak "gumming" season.

By 1850, the company of Curtis and Son had made enough money to move its office to Portland, Maine. This put the company closer to big cities, such as Boston, which

In 1869, William F. Semple, a dentist from Mount Vernon, Ohio, obtained the first patent for what he called an "improved chewing-gum." Dr. Semple planned to make his gum out of rubber, adding "scouring-properties" such as chalk, powdered licorice root, and charcoal. He believed his gum would exercise the jaws and clean the teeth at the same time. Dr. Semple was known for his painful extractions, so perhaps it's just as well he never bothered to manufacture his chewing gum!

would help increase sales. John reasoned it was only a matter of time before State of Maine Pure Spruce Gum would be sold in every city in America.

Courtesy John Wardlaw

Recipe For Success

The spruce gum of yesteryear was quite different from our chewing gum of today.

First, it came in only one color, its natural one: pinkish tan.

Second, people found it hard to chew. It could cause a splitting jaw-ache.

Third, the flavor was sharp, not sweet. Robert Hendrickson, in *The Great American Chewing Gum Book*, compares his first bite of spruce gum to "sinking your teeth into frozen gasoline." If you can last long enough, says Hendrickson, the gasoline flavor mellows to a tangy or woodsy taste. Many people today find it refreshing. Others find it disgusting. Either way, the flavor lasts for hours.

The process for making gum in the mid-nineteenth century was also very different from today's factory production lines. Here is an 1840s recipe for Curtis and Son's State of Maine Pure Spruce Gum:

> **Step One:** Throw gobs of raw spruce resin into a big kettle—bark and all!
> **Step Two:** Bring resin to a boil.
> **Step Three:** Skim off bark, twigs, and other impurities as they rise to the top of the kettle.
> **Step Four:** Stir boiling resin until it thickens like molasses.
> **Step Five:** While still hot, pour gum onto a slab and roll out into a flat sheet about 1/4 inch thick.
> **Step Six:** Chop into strips about 1/2 inch wide and 3/4 inch long.
> **Step Seven:** Dip gum strips into cornstarch to keep them from sticking.
> **Step Eight:** Pack twenty strips of gum to a box.

FROM RAGS TO RICHES

By 1850, the market for State of Maine Pure Spruce Gum had grown larger than ever. John invented several machines to produce his gum faster and more efficiently. He hired 200 employees, who processed 1,800 boxes of gum a day. He added other gums to his line, with names such as Yankee Spruce, American Flag, 200 Lump Spruce, and C.C.G. (thought to mean Curtis Chewing Gum). At one point, John wrote a check for the amount of $35,000, enough to buy 20,000 pounds—ten tons—of raw gum. (That's the weight of four small rhinoceroses!) No one has ever broken that record.

Curtis and Company also manufactured gums made of paraffin, the same wax used in candles. Paraffin wasn't a great gum. It needed the warmth and saliva of a person's mouth to make it munchable. Plus, after chewing it for long periods, people found that it disintegrated, leaving them with wax slivers stuck in their teeth. But Curtis and Company discovered how to add vanilla flavoring and sugar to the paraffin. Customers loved the sweetened "chaws," even though the flavor faded fast. Curtis paraffin gums such as "Licorice Lulu," "Biggest and Best," "Four-in-Hand," and "Sugar Cream" disappeared from shopkeepers' shelves as fast as they could stock them.

Paraffin gum is a mineral wax made by distilling crude oil. The translucent wax that remains is tasteless and odorless, and molds well into a variety of shapes. Today, you can buy chewable, sweetened paraffin gum formed to look like Dracula teeth, ruby-red lips, witch fingernails, and other novelty items.

The Maine Forest Service estimates that over 150 tons of raw spruce gum were harvested every year in the mid-1800s (worth about $300,000). Other experts say it's possible workers gathered closer to *1,500* tons annually.

White Mountain became the most popular paraffin gum of all. Rolled like a pencil, about three inches long, and wrapped in colored tissue paper, it became the first gum ever to sell in a fancy package. Other paraffin gums would later boast of containing "picture cards," the parent of today's bubble gum cards.

By 1852, John's prediction had come true. People could buy Curtis and Son gum in almost any city in America. Wealthy beyond their dreams, John and his father moved their company once more, this time into a three-story building. They called it the Curtis Chewing Gum Factory—the first chewing gum factory in the world.

EXTRA! EXTRA! READ ALL ABOUT IT!

In the late 1800s, the boom of spruce gum finally went bust. The newspaper industry had expanded, requiring more wood pulp from the New England forests to keep the presses rolling. As lumberjacks cut down more trees, raw spruce became scarce. By the 1930s, most spruce gum manufacturers had closed their doors. The novelty of chomping wild resin faded. People wanted a softer, sweeter chew. Spruce gum now sold only in out-of-the-way shops in the deep woods of Maine.

John Bacon Curtis might not have minded. He died in 1897, rich in money and in the knowledge that he had pioneered a new industry that would eventually spread throughout the world.

"Remember The Alamo!": General López De Santa Anna And Thomas Adams

"[Genies] belong to whoever rubs the lamp [said Tom Sawyer] . . .
and they've got to do whatever he says. If he tells them to build a palace
forty miles long, out of di'monds, and fill it full of chewing gum . . . they've got to do it.
. . . I thought all this over for two or three days, and then I reckoned
I would see if there was anything in it. I got an old tin lamp . . .
and rubbed and rubbed . . . but it warn't no use, none of the genies come."
—Huck Finn in *The Adventures of Huckleberry Finn*,
by Mark Twain, 1884

Two men.

One, a power-hungry dictator and hated military general with a false leg.

The other, an orphan who worked as a photographer and struggled to become a successful inventor.

The first man was responsible for the massacre at the Alamo.

23

The second man isn't famous. But almost every kid in America has chewed his most famous invention.

General Antonio López de Santa Anna and Mr. Thomas Adams. Two very different men leading very different lives. But when their paths crossed in 1869, they changed the future—and shape—of chewing gum forever.

"VICTORY OR DEATH"

Early in the morning of March 6, 1836, General Santa Anna ordered 1,500 soldiers to attack the Alamo, a small mission in San Antonio, Texas. Santa Anna wanted to punish the rebels inside the fortress for proclaiming their independence from Mexico.

The 188 Texans were proud of their new country. Although outnumbered, they vowed to fight to the end. "I shall never surrender nor retreat," said Colonel William B. Travis, the Alamo's commander. "I am determined . . . to die like a soldier who never forgets what is due to his honor and that of his country. Victory or death."

Santa Anna told a bugler to sound a battle cry. "Show no mercy. Take no prisoners," he commanded. Within an hour, the Alamo had been overrun. Every Texan lay dead.

A few weeks later, another bugle sounded. This time, it belonged to Texas. With inspiring cries of "Remember the Alamo!" General Sam Houston's troops charged Santa Anna's army. After a victorious battle, Houston took Santa Anna prisoner. He agreed to let the Mexican general go free under one condition: Santa Anna must sign a treaty recognizing the independence of Texas.

The newly formed country of Texas remained in existence for only nine years. In 1845 it became the twenty-eighth state of the United States.

Reluctantly, the general signed. He returned to Mexico, ready to resume his prewar position as president. But the Mexican government was furious at his surrender. They exiled him to Cuba, where he lived for ten years. Later, Santa Anna immigrated to the United States, moving to Staten Island. But he never gave up his secret plan: to return to Mexico and regain his power.

Chance Encounter

Meanwhile, in New York City, a middle-aged man named Thomas Adams lived with his wife and seven children.

Orphaned at the age of nine, Adams had learned to be self-sufficient. He had worked hard to make something of his life.

During the American Civil War, Adams served as a military photographer. He took hundreds of formal portraits of uniformed men, which the soldiers sent home to their families to become precious keepsakes.

But Adams didn't find photography challenging enough. He had a quick, sharp mind, and soon took to inventing a variety of gadgets and gimmicks. His horsefeed bag and a special burner for kerosene lamps sold well. But most of his inventions failed.

Restless and discouraged, Adams bought a glass shop in 1869, one block from the Staten Island ferry dock. He settled there, determined to support his family. Yet he never gave up his dream to become a successful inventor.

One day, a man named Rudolph Napegy entered Adams's store to ask about an item in the display window. He and Adams struck up a conversation. Napegy enjoyed talking with the ingenious inventor and visited the glass shop many times.

Eventually, Napegy asked if he could introduce Adams to his boss. The boss held the key to a new invention; perhaps Adams would enjoy unlocking it? Napegy assured the inventor that if successful, he would become a very wealthy man.

Adams agreed to the meeting. On a sunny morning in 1869, he and his oldest son rode the Staten Island ferry to the home of Napegy's boss, former general Antonio López de Santa Anna.

"TREASURE OF MEXICO"

The ex-general was now seventy-five years old, white-haired, and partially deaf. Yet he still carried himself with the arrogance and intensity of a fanatical warrior. He told Adams he needed to raise money—enough to fund an entire army. He alone would lead the march to overthrow the Mexican government.

"I shall be *presidente* again!" Santa Anna proclaimed. He ordered Napegy to bring out a bag. "We can make millions, Señor Adams. Millions, millions of dollars! Here is the treasure of Mexico." He emptied the bag's contents onto a table.

Adams stared at what looked like a large lump of dirt, covered with bark and pebbles. At this moment, he may have wondered if Santa Anna was crazy.

But the ex-general explained, "This is chicle, the latex of the sapodilla tree, which we have in great abundance in my country." Santa Anna knew that crude rubber, used for carriage and bicycle tires, sold for a dollar a pound. Chicle sold for only five cents a pound. If Adams could devise a way to convert the springy sap into a cheap rubber substitute, the invention would indeed earn them millions.

The more Adams heard about chicle, the more he grew excited. Chicle could revolutionize the rubber industry. Adams immediately imported a ton of the substance from Santa Anna's supporters in Mexico. With the help of his four sons, he began secret experiments at home.

Several months passed. Adams ruined every cooking pot in his wife's kitchen. Yet he grew no closer to creating a chicle-based rubber. Santa Anna grew impatient, and then angry. Finally, he lost interest altogether and disappeared from Adams's life. The inventor was left with a warehouse full of chicle and a stubborn determination to continue his experiments.

"ADAMS' NEW YORK NO. 1 – SNAPPING AND STRETCHING"

Adams spent the next year boiling and bubbling the chicle. He enlisted the help of several friends, including a chemist, but nothing worked. No matter what he did to the chicle, he couldn't make it react like rubber: It had no flexibility, no resilience, no bounce. And it often shredded in his hands.

"[My father] had about made up his mind to throw the whole lot into the East River," recalled Adams's son, Horatio. "But it so happened that before this was done, [he] went into a drugstore . . . to purchase something. While he was there, a little girl came in and asked for a penny's worth of chewing gum."

Adams knew that many Mexicans—including Santa Anna—enjoyed chewing chicle. Adams and his sons had often munched chunks of the springy stuff during their experiments. Perhaps the warehouse full of chicle could be salvaged after all! As Horatio remembered:

> "After the child left the store, [my father] asked the druggist what kind of chewing gum the little girl had bought. He was told that it was made of paraffin wax, was called White Mountain, and was 'pretty poor gum.' When he asked the man if he would be willing to try an entirely different kind of gum, the druggist agreed. When [my father] arrived home that night, he spoke to . . . Tom, Jr., my oldest brother, about his idea. Junior was very much impressed and suggested that they make up a few boxes of chicle chewing gum. . . ."

That evening, Adams and his sons set to work.

"My father and I took some chicle and put it into hot water," said Horatio, who was sixteen years old at the time. "We left it there until it was about the consistency of putty. Then we wet our hands, rubbed and kneaded it and finally rolled it into little balls—two hundred of them. It was no longer brownish black, but a kind of grayish white." The family had just invented the first gum balls.

Adams priced the gum at two for a penny, and sent a three-month supply to his druggist friend. In February 1871, the gum went on sale in New Jersey. Kids who stopped by the store on their way to school loved the tasteless, taffylike chaw. By noon the first day, every piece had sold out.

Encouraged by this success, Adams and his boys invested thirty-five dollars—all the money they had—in more gum. They cooked up a smoother batch, this time flattening it into little sticks. Then they wrapped the gum in brightly colored tissue paper. Two hundred sticks went into a box featuring a color picture of New York's City Hall. They called the gum Adams' New York No.1—Snapping and Stretching.

Adams' Red Rose Healthy Pure Chewing Gum was packaged in elaborate wrappings and said to be flavored with "the finest oil of peppermint."

On The Road Again

Tom, Jr., thought the best way to sell Adams' New York No. 1 was by taking it on the road—just as John B. Curtis had twenty years earlier. Since Tom already worked as a traveling salesman, he offered to carry twenty-five boxes of gum on his next journey west.

Weeks later, Tom returned home with all twenty-five boxes still in hand. Not a single druggist could be convinced to buy the new gum.

Although many people enjoyed chewing gum during the late 1800s, others did not approve of the habit. If you were caught chewing chicle in school, a teacher might rap your knuckles hard with a ruler. On stage, an actress playing the role of an evil woman chewed gum as proof of that character's wickedness. And scientists spread false rumors that chicle was a mixture of horses' hooves and glue! If you accidentally swallowed the gum, they claimed, your intestines would stick together, causing instant death.

"Determination" was the family's middle name, however. Tom carried the gum on his next sales trip. This time, he vowed not to bring the boxes home. If shopkeepers didn't want to buy the new product, he would let them sell it on consignment: The druggists would pay Tom only if the gum sold.

The arrangement worked. John arrived home to find his father had already received orders for three hundred boxes of gum.

Thrilled, Tom quit his job. He and his father decided to go into the chewing gum business full-time. They formed a company called Adams and Sons. Then they rented a small building and hired twenty-five young women to wrap and box the sticks of gum. Tom's former boss was skeptical but kind. "If you fail, which I think you will," he warned, "you may have your job back with me."

But Adams and Sons did *not* fail. By late 1871, sales boomed. Adams invented a new gum-making machine, which kneaded the chicle like dough and then flattened it into thin strips. The machine also notched each strip so that a druggist could easily break off a penny's worth of gum for customers.

Soon, Adams began experimenting with flavored chicle gum. Chicle itself does not absorb flavors, so Adams added the dried root bark from the sassafras tree. In another experiment, he shredded licorice into the chicle, which turned the gum black. He gave it the name Black Jack. You can still buy it today.

Black Jack wasn't the only flavored gum available. By 1879, John Colgan, a pharmacist in Kentucky, had heard about Adams's success. He, too, experimented with chicle, discovering that its flavors lasted longer if he mixed the gum with powdered sugar.

A one-ton shipment of chicle was soon to arrive in Kentucky from Central America. Colgan ordered 100 pounds of it. But when the chicle was delivered, he found he had to buy the entire ton—or none at all. Colgan gulped, but purchased the gum. He mixed it with sugar and with tolu, a fragrant, spicy sap used in cough syrup and perfume.

Colgan's Taffy-Tolu Chewing Gum became an overnight sensation in 1880. Colgan sold his drug-store and started a gum manufacturing plant. He hired boys to carry his product in baskets, hawking it on the streets and aboard horse trolleys. Within a year, ten other companies were making the popular tolu-flavored gum.

Tutti-Frutti

By the 1880s, the entire United States was "stuck" on chewing gum. Adams and Sons became so successful that they opened a six-story factory with more than 250 employees. Part of the company's success stemmed from another of Adams's great inventions: the chewing gum vending machine. Adams set up his machines along the elevated-train platforms in New York City. He filled them with Tutti-Frutti, his colorful gum balls made with a mixture of sweet fruit flavors. Later, Adams printed slogans about his new product on small signs along Broadway, making Tutti-Frutti the first gum ever to be advertised.

Adams finally retired as president of Adams and Sons in 1899, at the age of eighty-one. He died six years later, leaving his family a fortune. (When Tom, Jr. died in 1926, his estate alone was worth $2 million—about $27 million today.) Thomas Adams had taken thirty-five dollars, a lump of dirt, and a dream—and turned them into a chewing gum empire. His chicle would become the base for all chewing gum for most of the twentieth century.

Perhaps today when you hear the phrase "Remember the Alamo!" you'll think of the brave men who fought and died there. Perhaps you'll also think of an innovative inventor by the name of Mr. Thomas Adams.

And what of General Antonio López de Santa Anna? He was eventually allowed to return to Mexico, but he never regained power. He died at the age of eighty-one—poor and forgotten.

CHAPTER
4

THE CHEWING GUM KING:
WILLIAM WRIGLEY, JR.

One, two—it's good to chew,
Three, four—they all want more,
Five, six—it comes in sticks,
Seven, eight—the flavor's great,
Nine, ten—gum again!
IT'S WRIGLEY'S.
—from a "*Mother Goose*" booklet,
published by Wrigley's Chewing Gum, 1915

He never wore a crown or royal robe. He never carried a scepter or ruled from a throne. Yet he built a skyscraper that resembled a palace and reigned over his company like a proud king. He named this empire after himself: the William Wrigley, Jr., Company. Today, more than sixty years after his death—100 years after he introduced his world-famous Wrigley's Spearmint gum—the company he created still rules as Number One.

William Wrigley, Jr., didn't start out like a king. By age eleven, Wrigley was being expelled from school about once every three weeks. He had a dynamic personality: bright, brash, bold. But he was also often bored and restless, especially in school. Teachers wrote many letters to his father, complaining about the boy's rebelliousness. Finally, Wrigley had enough. In 1873, the summer before seventh grade, he ran away to New York City.

With his last nickel, Wrigley bought several newspapers and set up shop as a newsie, a boy who hawks papers on the streets. His bed was the grating outside a newspaper building. When the presses rolled, heat seeped up through the air ducts to warm him. On rainy nights, he slept under parked horse-wagons, using newspapers as his blanket.

When Wrigley tired of this harsh life, he decided to become a sailor. He had no trouble getting hired as a seaman, but hated his job peeling potatoes in the galley. At summer's end he jumped ship and made his way back home.

His father, the owner of a soap factory, was happy to see his eldest son. He enrolled Wrigley in school again, with high hopes that the boy had changed. Wrigley hadn't. One

In the 1890s Wrigley's gum was delivered to shopkeepers by horse-drawn wagon.

Courtesy Wm. Wrigley Jr. Company

day, in eighth grade, he threw a cream pie at the school's nameplate. He was expelled again—for the last time.

"Your school life hasn't been a success," his father said. But what else could be done with this unruly boy? Wrigley, Sr., had eight other children to worry about. He had no time or patience for a child gone bad. So he handed Wrigley a paddle and ordered him to work at the soap factory. The twelve-year-old had the toughest job in the plant: stirring vats of thick, steaming soap.

CLEANING UP HIS ACT

For the next year, Wrigley worked ten hours a day, six days a week. He earned only six dollars a month. But he never complained. Instead, he stirred, planned, and waited.

When Wrigley turned thirteen, he begged his father to promote him to traveling salesman. "You're too young," said Wrigley, Sr. But his son's newfound drive and determination had impressed him.

The young Wrigley got his promotion. Equipped with a wagon and team of four horses, he traveled happily throughout Pennsylvania, New York, and New England. People liked the handsome, blue-eyed boy. He had a knack for good conversation and he bent over backwards to make his customers happy. He cajoled even the grouchiest of shopkeepers to buy from him. Wrigley, Sr., beamed with pride. For the next sixteen years, the former grammar school dropout ruled as the company's top salesman.

SOMETHING FOR NOTHING

In 1891, at the age of twenty-nine, Wrigley decided to go into business for himself. He was earning only ten dollars a week working for his father. Perhaps on his own he could do better.

By this time, Wrigley had married his childhood sweetheart. He and his wife packed up and left Philadelphia. With thirty-two dollars in his pocket, Wrigley opened his own soap company in Chicago.

During his years on the road, Wrigley had learned a clever sales gimmick: Shopkeepers often bought more of his product if they could also get something for nothing. As incentive to buy his new soap, Wrigley offered premiums—prizes or rewards—with each order. The shopkeepers could either use the premiums themselves, or sell them to customers, keeping all the profit.

The first premiums Wrigley offered were cheap umbrellas. Later, he tried razors, scales, and women's purses. The most successful premium was a simple can of baking powder. In fact, merchants liked the baking powder better than the soap. Soon Wrigley stopped selling soap altogether and became a baking powder salesman. With each ten-cent can of powder, he offered two free packs of gum. To his surprise, customers now preferred gum to the baking powder.

That's when Wrigley made the most important decision of his life: He would start a chewing gum business.

First, Wrigley studied the gum market, learning two things. One: People preferred chicle to spruce or paraffin gum. Two: Women chewed more gum than men.

Wrigley enjoyed spending money on himself, especially since he had worked so hard for it. But he also enjoyed spending it on his employees. He offered free medical care, life insurance, laundry services, and opened a staff cafeteria. He was the first employer to give workers Saturdays off, and once a month paid for free manicures and shampoos for his female employees.

With these facts in mind, Wrigley placed an order with the Zeno Gum Company in 1892 for his first chicle-based gum. He called it Vassar after the New York women's college. Later that year, he added two other gums to his line: Lotta (for chewers who liked "a lotta gum") and Sweet Sixteen Orange, which pictured the sweet face of a teenage girl on the package. Juicy Fruit and Wrigley's Spearmint followed in 1893.

"Anybody can make gum," Wrigley said. "Selling

Wrigley introduced his "Mother Goose" booklets for children in 1915. The nursery rhymes and fanciful drawings were later used in a series of magazine advertisements in the 1920s.

it is the problem." And despite his background and know-how, selling *was* Wrigley's biggest problem. In the 1890s, a dozen major gum companies already existed in the United States. They featured well-known, popular gums such as Black Jack, Beeman's, and Yucatan.

But the tough market didn't frighten the future gum king. "Fear saps more men than almost anything else in the world," he explained. "There's nothing in life that can really hurt you except yourself." In the years that followed, Wrigley would go broke three times.

He would lose his offices twice to fire. But he refused to give up, and, after each setback, he quickly returned to giving the competition a run for its money.

"TELL 'EM QUICK AND TELL 'EM OFTEN"

In the early years, Wrigley kept his business afloat by continuing to offer premiums. Shopkeepers who stocked his gum had their choice of fountain pens, lamps, clocks, coffee mills, cameras, cash registers, guns, Indian hatchets, baby carriages, slot machines, and even free accident insurance.

Wrigley also devised new ways for merchants to promote his gum. For example, he encouraged restaurants to display his products next to the cash register. With their money already in hand, customers were tempted to spend a few cents more for a pack of gum.

Wrigley promoted his gum through advertising as well. Most gum companies advertised in a modest way, using small street signs or trolley car posters. Wrigley was a larger than life man, and believed that advertising should be larger than life, too. In 1906, he placed huge ads for his gum in every newspaper and on every billboard and streetcar in upstate New York. Sales skyrocketed.

Then in 1907, Wrigley dared to go further.

The U.S. economy was suffering a recession. To save money, companies all over the country canceled advertising plans. Not Wrigley's. "People chew harder when they are sad," he reasoned. He wheeled and dealed, begged and borrowed and, finally, scraped together enough money to buy $1.5 million worth of advertising. He also offered a free box of gum to every merchant who ordered from him.

The scheme was risky. Wrigley could have lost everything. But in one year, sales for his gum soared from $170,000 to over $1 million. Wrigley bought more ads. Three years later, Wrigley's Spearmint was the most popular gum in America.

What was Wrigley's secret? "Get a good product," he said. Then "tell 'em quick, and tell 'em often . . . Advertising is pretty much like running a train. You've got to keep on

One of the greatest and most famous advertisements of all time was Wrigley's mile-long sign.

shoveling coal into the engine . . . [otherwise], it will . . . come to a dead stop."

The most creative advertising ploy Wrigley thought up was his Mother Goose booklet. In 1915, he had a variety of nursery rhymes rewritten to feature his gum. These were published in a booklet, illustrated with the "Sprightly Spearmen," Wrigley's Spearmint elves. Here are three samples of the rhymes:

> Jack be nimble
> Jack be quick
> Jack run and get your
> Wrigley stick!
>
> As I was going to St. Ives
> I met a man with seven wives,

Each wife had a fine clear skin,
All were fat—not one was thin,
And each had a dimple in her chin:
What caused it?—WRIGLEY'S!

Don't sing a song of sixpence
A nickel is enough!
And when you bake the blackbirds
If you should find them tough
Just get a pack of Double Mint
Let everybody sing:
"Wrigley's after every meal
Is just the very thing!"

Along with silly rhymes, the Mother Goose booklet included information about the "healthfulness" of Wrigley's products. A doctor urged readers to "have plenty of chewing gum on hand" to aid their digestion. Experts also reminded the public that gum could calm nerves, relieve thirst, ease a scratchy throat, freshen breath, and increase appetite. From 1915 to 1917, Wrigley gave away over 14 million of his Mother Goose booklets, which he dedicated "to the children of the world—from [ages] 6 to 60."

Here are some other inventive ways Wrigley told the American public "quick and often":

• He bought advertising space on 62,000 street and subway cars.

• He erected a giant, flashing Wrigley's sign that towered over New York City's Times Square. The annual electric bill came to $104,000.

• He sent free samples of gum to people listed in American telephone books. In all, over 8.5 million people received the freebies.

•He mailed two free sticks of gum to two-year-olds on their birthdays; 750,000 kids received these 'birthday presents' every year.

•He created the first singing commercials, or jingles, for radio. Later, he sponsored a radio program called *The Lone Wolf,* where listeners could join an "Indian tribe." Over six hundred thousand children signed up.

During his lifetime, Wrigley spent over $100 million advertising his gum. He is known today as a pioneer—one of the first to use ads to increase sales of brand-name products.

•He built the most famous Wrigley advertisement of all time: a "mile-long" sign that followed the tracks of a New Jersey railroad. The sign looked like a boxcar train, with 117 posters chained together. Each poster was a lookalike gum wrapper advertising a different flavor. The sign also featured the Wrigley sprite, an elflike creature with a pointy head.

Over the years, Wrigley became a multimillionaire. He bought several cars, all red, "so I can find them," he said. He also bought the Chicago Cubs baseball team (Wrigley Field, where the Cubs play, is named after him) and Catalina, an island off the coast of California. He hired an architect to design his company skyscraper to look like a birthday cake with finger tracings in the icing. He built a special aviary on Catalina and filled it with six thousand birds. And the money kept pouring in.

Yet it was his work that Wrigley loved best. He got up at five A.M. every morning, anxious to greet the day. And he stayed up late every night, hating to see the day end. "Making money doesn't amount to a hill of beans," he once said in his booming voice. "The only real joy in business is in the joy of creating. Nothing is so much fun as business."

When he died in 1932, at age seventy, Wrigley was one of the ten wealthiest men in America. His kingdom stretched to thirty-seven countries. His factories produced 280

By 1914, enough gum was bought in the United States each year for every single person to have thirty-nine pieces. Today, Americans buy six times that amount.

millions sticks of gum a week. Today, the Wm. Wrigley Jr. Company has thirteen factories and sells its products in 119 countries. His gum is the most famous in the world.

THE FIRST BUBBLERS: FRANK H. FLEER AND WALTER DIEMER

*Jolly Van Pelt wore a pink warm-up suit. First she did a
bunch of jumping jacks. Then she pulled out a skipping
rope and jumped in place. . . .*

*"What's the big idea, Jolly?" I asked. "This is a bubble gum
blowing contest, not an aerobics workout."*

*"I'm toning up," she snapped. "It's not against the rules."
She did two quick knee bends. "Ready," she said.
I shook my head. Maybe that was why I couldn't blow bubbles.
I never did the warm-up stuff.*

    —Busy O'Brien and the Great Bubble Gum Blowout,
     by Michelle Poploff, 1990

Office workers huddled around him, watching, waiting. He knew what they were thinking: Would he do it? *Could* he do it?

He stuffed a thick, sugary wad into his mouth. He chomped. He chewed. Then he poked his tongue into the center of the chunk . . . and blew.

People held their breath.

The bubble grew.

Everyone's eyes grew wide.

The bubble grew. It rose higher and higher, like a balloon tugging against a string, ready to float on the breeze. And still it grew. Until . . .

POP!

He'd done it. The year was 1928, and twenty-three-year-old Walter Diemer had just invented the world's first bubble gum.

Bubbles Or Bust

The story of the first bubble actually begins forty years earlier, long before Diemer popped into the history books.

In the late nineteenth century, gum chewing in America was fast becoming more than just a passing fad. Many businessmen, such as William Wrigley, Jr., and Thomas Adams, knew the gum craze was here to stay. Another businessman with foresight was Frank H. Fleer. For years, he had worked for his father-in-law, Otto Holstein, in a factory that manufactured flavorings for candy. In 1880 Holstein turned the business over to Fleer. With his background in flavorings and candy sales, Fleer was able to change the factory into a chewing gum company. He began producing gum in 1885.

Most bubble gum today is made from synthetic ingredients, such as vinyl resins or microcrystalline waxes. But Walter Diemer's formula used only natural ingredients. His recipe included a rubbery latex similar to chicle. This latex was very much like the "rubber" used in the 1920s to make women's girdles!

Competition would be tough. Dozens of gums already flavored the market. Fleer knew that many doctors believed chewing gum could relax facial nerves and muscles. Perhaps Fleer could make a gum that was both healthful *and* fun. After much consideration, he set about creating a gum that could be blown into large bubbles.

Not an easy task. The usual gum bases lacked "bubbleability." Spruce had the jaw-tiring thickness of taffy. Chicle was too sticky. And paraffin gum just wouldn't blow, period. So Fleer began experiments to produce a synthetic gum base.

BLIBBER-BLUBBER

Bubble gum differs from regular gum in two ways. First, it needs a high surface tension. This means it must have enough strength to hold its balloon shape as air stretches the bubble thinner and thinner. Without this strength, the gum is too brittle to hold much air. A bubble will break before it has a chance to grow.

Second, bubble gum needs a higher "snap-back," or elasticity. Try this experiment: Hold a rubber band with both hands and gently stretch it, but not too far. Now release one end. The rubber band snaps back instantly to its original shape.

Quality bubble gum should react the same way. With low snap-back, a bubble will pop over your chin and nose. With high snap-back, most of the gum will return to your lips, ready for another bubble.

For more than twenty years, Fleer experimented with a variety of formulas, all without success. But he refused to let his dream bubble burst. Finally, in 1906, the Frank H. Fleer Corporation unveiled the first bubble gum ever. Fleer himself gave it the tongue-tripping name Blibber-Blubber.

The gum was an instant disaster. It tasted great. And it could bubble, all right. But the stuff was too brittle. Bubbles would explode without warning. Also, they had the messy habit of sticking to the blower's face. The only way to remove it from someone's skin was by scrubbing it with turpentine. Fleer had to admit that he'd botched his batch: Blibber-Blubber was a major blunder.

In The Pink

Years passed. Fleer went on to market different flavors of regular chewing gum. In 1910 he invented Chiclets, a gum modeled after the candy-coated almonds popular during that time. But he never stopped searching for a true bubble gum. Even after his death, Fleer's chemists continued their experiments, this time under the supervision of his son-in-law, Gilbert Mustin.

The first pinkish-colored gum was invented in 1899 by Franklin V. Canning, the manager of a drugstore in New York City. Canning's gum was also the first to be promoted as an aid to oral hygiene. "Prevents decay, sweetens breath," read the package. "The Gum That Cleans the Teeth." Canning called his new gum Dentyne—a combination of the words "dental" and "hygiene."

Then came the fateful day.

Walter Diemer was a young accountant at the Fleer Corporation. He learned of Mustin's search for the perfect bubble gum and decided to pitch in. He worked at home for over a year, mixing his own batches of bubbly brew. He didn't know any chemistry. His method, he explained later, was "simple trial and error."

But his work paid off. On an early-August morning in 1928, Diemer brought his latest five-pound batch of gum to work. Then, as the office staff watched, he blew a small bubble. It kept growing. And growing. No one had ever seen anything like it. Best of all, when it finally popped, it was a soft pop—and Diemer peeled it easily off his nose.

"I had it!" Diemer recalled thinking. "Everybody tried some. It really went to our heads. We were blowing bubbles and dancing all over the office!"

The celebration didn't last long. By the next morning, Diemer's new gum "wouldn't blow worth a darn." Not a bubble, not a blip. No one could figure out why, so Diemer went back to the drawing board.

Four months later, a few days before Christmas, Diemer tried again. This time he used one of the company vats and mixed *three hundred pounds* of his new recipe.

"I was young," he later recalled, "very self-conscious, and all the help was standing around looking very skeptical. . . . They just stared disapprovingly and I was certain they were all thinking, *That crazy kid. That stuff he made is going to break the blades in our mixing machines.* Well, the machines started groaning, and the mix started popping and then . . . I realized I'd forgotten to put any coloring in the gum!"

The new gum bubbled just fine. But despite its sweetness, no one wanted to chew the unappetizing gray mass. Diemer scrapped the first batch and made a new batch of the bubbly stuff the very next day. Pink food coloring was the only kind on hand, so he grabbed a bottle and dumped the bright liquid into the monstrous vat. "And that's the reason . . ." he admitted, "that bubble gum has [always] been . . . pink!"

DECK THE HALLS WITH . . . DUBBLE BUBBLE?

Diemer's boss was thrilled with the new invention. He named it Dubble Bubble and decided to test-market it immediately. Diemer found some old taffy-wrapping machines in Atlantic City for packaging the gum. The day after Christmas, Dubble Bubble went on sale in a small mom-and-pop candy shop in Philadelphia. The Fleer Corporation also handed out free samples to drug and grocery stores.

The pink "Christmas present" was an overnight sensation. Kids and adults loved it. Unfortunately, other gum companies loved it, too. Diemer hadn't bothered to get a patent for his invention, fearing it would expose his secret recipe. But his plan backfired. Within three months, several manufacturers had analyzed his ingredients and their imitations were soon available in almost every store.

But none of the copy-bubbles was as good as Diemer's original. By the end of 1929, Dubble Bubble had passed Tootsie Rolls to become the world's best-selling one-cent treat.

During the roaring twenties, Americans bought 700 million pounds of chewing gum a year. That cost them about $100 million, or more than $2 million a week.

Today, Fleer's company produces more than five million pieces of Dubble Bubble *a day*, and exports it to over fifty countries around the world. It comes in a variety of flavors and colors—although pink still seems to be everyone's favorite. When you hear the words "bubble gum," you probably picture that little pink pillow that Walter Diemer made so famous seventy years ago.

And what about Walter Diemer? He worked at the Fleer Corporation for forty-three years and was promoted to senior vice-president. He could have become a billionaire if only he'd have gotten a patent for his recipe. But as the first bubbler approached age ninety, he said he had no regrets. "Bubble gum brought a little happiness to millions of kids," he commented. "And if I could do that, I'm happy."

THE CLOWN PRINCE OF BUBBLE GUM: J. WARREN BOWMAN

> "Hey, Teresa, how's the gum chewing?" [Jeffrey asked.]
> Teresa wrinkled her nose. "Awful. I've been chewing this same
> piece of bubble gum for seven-and-a-half weeks, and it's as hard
> as my binder. Tastes about as good, too."
> Teresa was shooting for the World's Record for the Longest Chew
> of One Piece of Bubble Gum. . . .
> "My jaws are killing me," Teresa said, "but I only have to suffer
> three more days before I beat the record set by that girl in Oklahoma.
> She accidentally swallowed her gum one night when she was asleep.
> I keep mine tucked under my tongue. Feels weird, but works every time."
> —from *Operation Rhinoceros,* by Lee Wardlaw, 1992

Police officer. Doughnut vendor. Tropical-fruit hauler. Used-car salesman. Green turtle-egg hunter. Bubble gum manufacturer.

Question: Which of these jobs did J. Warren Bowman choose as his career?

Answer: All of them!

But, it wasn't until Bowman entered the world of bubble gum that he finally became a success. This success, combined with his wacky, flashy ways, earned him the nickname the Clown Prince of Bubble Gum, also known as King Bub.

Here's how the Clown Prince began his bubble buffoonery.

STEP RIGHT UP!

J. Warren Bowman was a big man, in both size and personality. He stood six foot three, weighed 220 pounds, and always spoke in a booming voice. He was also a born huckster. Like the infamous P. T. Barnum, circus showman of the 1800s, Bowman could sell anything to anyone. Several times during his years as a used-car salesman, he sold parked cars right off the street. Then he'd have to scramble to find their owners to convince them he'd just made the deal of the century.

Bowman's hero was another flamboyant man: William Wrigley, Jr. Inspired by Wrigley's success, Bowman traveled to Chicago to see his idol's skyscraper. He stood on the sidewalk beneath the Wrigley Building, staring up in awe. He stared for a long time; so long that a policeman grew suspicious and finally asked Bowman to leave.

Bubble gum . . . murder? The popular sampling campaigns of the 1930s gave one demented person a fiendish idea. On a June evening in 1934, Mrs. Georgia McKenzie of Sacramento, California, came home to find an envelope on her doorstep containing four free samples of gum. Mrs. McKenzie popped a piece into her mouth, and tasted a strange bitter flavor. She spit the gum out instantly and called the police. Authorities analyzed the samples and announced Mrs. McKenzie had been very lucky. They discovered the gum had been laced with enough poison to kill a dozen people! Although other homes in the neighborhood had also received gum samples, only the McKenzie gum was poisoned. Police suspected someone had plotted to kill Mrs. McKenzie, her mother and two teenage sons. No one ever learned why, and to this day the would-be murderer's identity remains a mystery.

Around 1929, Bowman lost a job with the police force. He had only twenty-five dollars in his pocket, but with slick salesmanship he persuaded a bank to loan him three hundred dollars. Then, he scrounged some old machines, bought barrels of sugar and glucose, and opened the Bowman Chewing Gum Company.

BY GOSH AND BY GUM

Bowman first made a regular brand called By Gum. It sold well, but not well enough to compete with other manufacturers.

Before the 1930s, chewing gum had sold as a seasonal product. Drugstore owners offered gum only between late spring and fall, the same period they kept their soda fountains open for business.

But times changed. "People chew harder when they are sad," the wise Wrigley had said. That was especially true during the Great Depression. During the 1930s, Americans pinched pennies even for bare necessities. Yet somehow, they always managed to afford a penny-stick of gum, and the market boomed.

To ensure the boom didn't go bust, many of Bowman's competitors increased their advertising and promotional activities.

For example, American Chicle Company, which then made Blackjack, Dentyne, and Clove gum, hired young women to work as "sampling girls." Dressed in orange satin costumes, the women offered free samples of gum to people on the streets of New York City. American Chicle told the girls to give away at least five thousand pieces of gum a day. In one year, more than 1.5 million New Yorkers sampled American Chicle's products. Sales skyrocketed.

The Wm. Wrigley Jr. Company also increased sales with a special promotional campaign. Wrigley's son, Philip, then president of the firm, wanted to learn why Americans enjoyed chewing gum. Across the country, pollsters dressed as the characters "Mr. Spear" and "Miss Mint" offered a whole dollar (a great deal of money in those days) to anyone who could answer Philip's question. Of course, the people surveyed also had to have open packs of Wrigley's Spearmint in their pockets. The poll ran from 1932 until 1935, with unanimous results. Gum chewing "relieves nervous tension," everyone said. Not a surprising answer during that difficult era.

Bowman admired these novel campaigns, but vowed not to be outdone. Instead, he jumped on the bubble bandwagon. Soon, his new gum Blony hit the market, advertised as the "biggest piece of gum available for a penny." Bowman boasted that kids chewing Blony could blow bubbles "twice as large as any other." The ads worked. Before long, Blony was Dubble Bubble's biggest and best competitor.

Nikola Tesla, the famous engineer and inventor of the alternating-current electrical system, had this to say about bubble gum in 1932: "By exhaustion of the salivary glands, gum puts many a foolish victim in the grave."

BUBBLE BLOOPER

The Clown Prince loved sales gimmicks—the more outlandish, the better. He borrowed many ideas from his gum hero, Wrigley the Great, including Wrigley's practice of offering premiums. Bowman gave his distributors coupons with every purchase. These coupons were redeemable for a variety of unusual items. Once, Bowman even awarded a customer a pedigree bull.

The premiums worked. Blony gum sales increased. When Bowman next included "picture cards" with every package—one of the first companies to do so—the ploy brought him fame. Unfortunately, this fame also created an international bubble gum blooper.

Originally, Bowman's bubble gum cards featured scenes with cowboys and Indians. Then he produced a startling, 240-card series picturing war heroes and battles. Americans happily snapped up more than 100 million of the "Horrors of War" cards. But the Japanese government didn't share that happiness.

In the early 1930s, Bowman had been the first person to build bubble gum factories in Japan. Parents and teachers there despised the gooey stuff. But kids loved it. They chewed it everywhere—and spit it out everywhere, too. Officials condemned this practice, claiming it was not only a "nuisance but also a menace to public health." Police in some cities were instructed to restrict or ban the gum chewing habit.

Japan's government also disapproved of Bowman's bubble gum cards. The empire had recently invaded China—an atrocity the cards highlighted. In 1937, Japanese Embassy officials in Washington complained hotly to the State Department. Japan was a peace-loving country, they stated, and demanded that Bowman right his wrong.

The State Department disagreed. Hadn't the Japanese government just sunk a U.S. gunboat on the Yangtze River (a fact documented on a Blony card)? The Embassy quietly withdrew its complaint, but immediately declared Bowman an "enemy of Japan." He and his factories were banished from the country forever.

The setback didn't upset the irrepressible King, who went on to produce the first eight-

stick package of gum. Later, he introduced another popular bubble gum called Bub. Sales continued to increase. After World War II, the Bowman Chewing Gum Company earned a million dollars a month selling Blony and Bub alone. At one point in his life, his products were selling four times as much as any other bubble gum on the market, including Dubble Bubble. Not bad for someone who had originally hunted green turtle eggs for a living.

Today, Blony, Bub, and By Gum no longer exist. The Topps Company bought out Bowman in 1954 and went on to manufacture another bubble gum. A bubble gum more popular than Blony or Fleer's Dubble Bubble. A gum with the wacky name of Bazooka. The Clown Prince of Bubble Gum would have been proud.

BUBBLE TROUBLE

I went to sleep with gum in my mouth and now there's gum in my hair . . . and I could tell that it was going to be a terrible, horrible, no good, very bad day.
　　　　—from *Alexander and the Terrible, Horrible, No Good,*
　　　　　　　　　　　　　　Very Bad Day by Judith Viorst, 1976

We can thank Walter Diemer for inventing bubble gum, but kids can take credit for turning it into a full-blown bubble boom.

In the years after bubble gum first hit the market, kids between the ages of three and fourteen chomped it by the chunkful. By 1941, children were buying $4.5 million worth of bubble gum a year. To meet the demand, more than twenty companies had started brewing their own brands. It looked as if American gum chewers would bubble happily ever after.

But then the bubble burst.

Despite its success, bubble gum was doomed to suffer its share of bubble trouble. And soon, it would disappear from the United States altogether.

BUBBLE GUM GOES TO WAR

President Roosevelt called December 7, 1941, "a date which will live in infamy." On that day, the Japanese bombed Pearl Harbor, destroying half of the United States Navy. Within twenty-four hours, American soldiers marched into World War II, armed with weapons, mess kits, survival gear . . . and chewing gum.

The U.S. military had learned just how valuable gum chewing could be during World War I. It freshened and cleansed the mouth when toothbrushes were unavailable. It quenched thirst when water was scarce. Most importantly, it relaxed soldiers during tense moments of fighting, increased their morale, and kept them alert—all of which helped save lives.

Now, more than twenty years later, gum had again become an essential part of a soldier's K rations. Before long, military mouths would chew almost six times more gum than civilians had chewed before the war. That meant 630 sticks a year—*per soldier.*

Not long after the United States entered the war, all the gum at Wrigley's Australian factory mysteriously disappeared. Later, it was learned the gum had been repackaged in wrappers that featured the U.S. and Philippines flags on one side. On the other side read the words of General MacArthur: "I shall return." Planes air-dropped thousands of this newly packaged gum to people trapped behind enemy lines in the Philippines.

In 1918, near the end of World War I, the American Red Cross shipped 4.5 million packs of chewing gum to France. The gum was used as a thirst quencher after the German Army, in retreat, poisoned many of the country's water systems.

American G.I.s chomped and popped their way across Europe, Africa, and Asia. They even introduced bubble gum to such remote places as Borneo, Pitcairn Island (where descendents of the *Bounty* mutineers still lived), and Alaska (which wasn't a state yet). Kids around the world learned the English phrase "Any gum, chum?" in hopes of begging a chaw when the Yanks came marching through town. In England and Australia, the slang word for American soldiers became "gum-chums."

But bubble gum wasn't just for bubbling. Almost every soldier has a story where bubble gum saved the day. Patches of gum repaired life rafts, machine guns, radio equipment, jeep tires, landing gear, and even submarines!

Bubble gum helps in civilian emergencies too. In 1988, a New York preschooler rammed a toy fire engine into a gas pipe, causing a dangerous leak. Luckily, his twelve-year-old baby-sitter kept cool—and plugged the leak with a wad of bubble gum!

BYE-BYE, BUBBLES

Back home, kids faced a sticky problem.

The war had caused a shortage of Siamese jelutong, the resin used in most bubble gums. Many factories were forced to shut down their operations at home, making only enough gum for the military. A few companies turned to synthetic resins for their bubble gum, but that didn't solve the problem for long. Sugar was also scarce. Since bubble gum is 60 percent sugar, even the synthetic brands soon disappeared from grocery store shelves.

During World War II, shortages of jelutong resin forced bubble gum companies to create the first gum base substitutes. Today, almost all bubble gum is made from synthetic resins, shipped to factories in large rectangular blocks.

Kids panicked. They stood in block-long lines for hours, waiting to shell out hard-earned nickels for one-cent wads of gum—even if they were stale.

After a few months, the only place to buy bubble gum was on the "pink market." Kids who had hoarded chunks at the beginning of the war now sold them illegally for up to a dollar each. Some clever children found a way to keep a precious piece of bubble gum fresh for almost a month. They plopped it in a glass of water every night before bed.

The war affected regular gum, too. Supplies of Central American chicle dried up. Sugar was rationed by the War Food Administration. So were peppermint and spearmint flavors, which flavored 90 percent of American gums. Manufacturers found they simply couldn't make enough quality gum for both soldiers and civilians. So civilians did without. It was the patriotic thing to do.

Meanwhile, Philip Wrigley hired a botanist to search the world for a plant that could provide a chicle substitute. The botanist found several, but not one was perfect. One of Philip's father's mottos had been: "Even in a little thing like a stick of gum, quality is important." Philip worried that the company's reputation might be damaged if it produced an inferior gum under the Wrigley label. On the other hand, he wanted to help the war effort.

During World War II, American gum factories produced and shipped more than 150 billion sticks of gum to soldiers overseas.

To solve his dilemma, Philip took Wrigley's Doublemint, Spearmint, and Juicy Fruit gums off the American market. In their place, the company produced a new gum under the label Orbit, advertising it as "a plain but honest wartime chewing gum."

A Pennsylvania man experienced the bubble gum boom personally in 1944 when a chunk he was chomping exploded in his mouth! He lost several teeth, but no one ever discovered how or why the gum exploded.

Although the gum tasted second-rate, Philip assured the public that it was still "pure and wholesome."

Civilians were so desperate for gum that even Orbit sold well. Stores that usually sold twenty packs of gum in two weeks now sold out in one or two days.

Philip Wrigley sent the company's entire production of famous gums overseas to the Armed Forces in 1944. But eventually, even soldiers had to chew Orbit. By 1945, supplies had become so scarce that Philip stopped production of every gum *except* Orbit. He also launched a unique advertising campaign. Ads appeared everywhere, displaying an empty wrapper of Wrigley's Spearmint Gum. The ads contained only three words: *Remember this wrapper!*

Americans did. After the war ended, Wrigley's Spearmint returned to the market in 1946, and the company regained its title as the king of chewing gums.

WHEN JOHNNY COMES BUBBLING HOME AGAIN

Victory!

The war ended. Men and women came marching home. Children cheered to see their families together again. They cheered almost as hard to see the return of bubble gum.

To celebrate, students in Longview, Texas, held a citywide bubble-blowing contest. They awarded prizes for bubbles with the loudest pop, the "most glamorous" shape, the "most geometric," as well as the messiest, smallest, largest, and cutest.

One school in New England even passed out wads to its students during final exams. It would help everyone relax and score higher on tests, school officials said.

Even working overtime, the gum manufacturers still couldn't keep up with the demand. Once again, block-long lines of kids formed outside stores, waiting for new shipments of "pink gold." The "pink market" prospered as it had during the war, with wads selling for a dollar a piece.

Slowly, the gum companies recovered. In 1946, a Texas candy importer named Andrew J. Paris managed to import five thousand tons of bubble gum from four Mexican factories. He became a hero to children everywhere, and *Life* magazine featured him on its cover. As Paris posed with a giant bubble eclipsing his mustache, the caption called him the "Man of Distinction" for America's kids.

In 1911, a British Royal Air Force dirigible (blimp) was halfway across the Atlantic Ocean when the crew discovered a leak in the water jacket of the engine. Quickly, they tried to patch it with glue and putty. Nothing worked. Desperate, Major H. C. Scott handed out packs of gum to his ten crew members, ordering them to chew "as if their lives . . . depended on it." And chew they did. Then they smeared the chewed wads over the leak, securing the mass with a strip of copper and bicycle tape and sealing the leak. Scott and his crew then knelt and "gave . . . thanks to the gum manufacturers."

Bubble gum's reputation strengthened, too. Since so many soldiers had chewed it during the war, many social taboos about gum crumbled away. Gum chewing increased 500 percent. And as long as kids chewed without too much snapping and popping, the habit became almost respectable.

THE BUBBLE GUM EPIDEMIC

Headaches. Sore throats. Vomiting.

In the summer of 1947, these flulike symptoms spread rapidly from one child to another until thousands fell ill across the nation. Doctors were mystified. What was causing this epidemic? Parents thought they knew the answer: bubble gum.

The U.S. Food and Drug Administration (FDA) decided to investigate. After collecting four thousand samples of bubble gum, officials began a series of scientific tests.

First, fifty adult and twenty-five child volunteers chomped and blew bubble gum for up to eight hours (some volunteers chewed six wads at a time). The results: volunteers showed no adverse symptoms—except achy jaws.

Next, scientists examined and analyzed the ingredients of the test wads. They implanted samples under the skin of guinea pigs and attached wads to shaved rabbits. Cats, dogs, monkeys, and chickens were fed the gum. Again, no negative reactions.

Finally, the FDA gave bubble gum a clean bill of health. The complaints were dismissed, the sick children recovered, and the "bubble gum epidemic" disappeared as mysteriously as it had come.

CHAPTER 8

GLOBS AROUND THE GLOBE

O Great Spirit of the Chewing Gum . . . we offer this prayer to thee.
There is grandeur in chewing gum. It is our marvelous pet, an important
accessory of mankind in this modern age. . . . It invites happiness. It attracts smiles.
An enjoyable and intellectual life is made possible because of gum chewing . . .
O Great Spirit of the Chewing Gum, rest in peace. . . .
—Japanese Shinto prayer, 1962

Kaugummi . . . zvykacka . . . mag farang . . . tsikles . . . shee yung tung!

Typographical errors? Klingon cuss words? The sounds your cat makes coughing up a furball?

Wrong.

This is what people call "chewing gum" in Germany, the Czech Republic, Thailand, Greece, and Malaysia.

A gum by any other name would chew as sweet. But no matter how you pronounce it, "gum" still translates to "fun" all over the world.

JOLLY GOOD GUM

In the nineteenth century a popcorn salesman from Cleveland, Ohio manufactured the first gum to achieve international fame. But a lack of good manners almost gummed up the works for his new product in England.

William White had tired of his job in the popcorn trade. An experienced candy maker, he decided to try operating a chewing gum factory. In 1876 he bought a plant that produced a paraffin-based gum called Busy Bee.

White made two important changes to improve the gum. First, he substituted chicle for paraffin to increase the chewability. Then, after many experiments on his kitchen stove, he learned how to combine chicle with corn syrup and peppermint to invent the first sweet, flavored, chicle-based gum. He named it Yucatan, hoping people would think they were chewing something exotic and romantic.

At first, the public didn't know *what* to think. Many people had never even tasted peppermint before. Using clever ads, White slowly educated chewers about the new flavor. Before long, Yucatan was a huge success. Dozens of companies producing nonflavored gum immediately went out of business. Only a few (such as Adams and Sons) saved themselves from bankruptcy by making sweet gum, too. Meanwhile, White scrambled to build a four-story factory and hire three hundred employees to manufacture more of his now-famous gum.

By 1893, 150 million sticks of Yucatan were selling every year. White was now a millionaire. He built a fifty-two–room mansion above Lake Erie. He bought a huge yacht called the *Say When*. And with a personality more flamboyant than either William Wrigley, Jr. or J. Warren Bowman, White got himself elected as a U.S. Congressman.

In 1918, at the end of World War I, England, France, Belgium, and Italy placed large orders for gum with American companies. Sales exceeded $2 million. Germany also placed an order for gum—for one whole dollar's worth! Later, the German government allowed an American company to set up a chewing gum factory in the city of Frankfurt. Taxes on the gum profits were then used to help make war reparations.

But after just one term in office, White grew weary of the political life. It was time again to do what he did best: Sell gum. In the early 1900s, he sailed the *Say When* to the British Isles, hoping to convince the English that Yucatan was "jolly good" gum.

Chewing gum had already captivated English children by the 1890s, a fact British parents weren't happy about. The *New York Daily Tribune* reprinted a news story from London in 1898 that read: "Health authorities here have issued a warning against the use of American chewing gum, which is fast becoming a rage among children of the East End. The authorities consider it more dangerous than the 'ice cream' which Italians sell in the street . . ."

These sentiments didn't stop White. He pulled a few strings and was granted an audience with England's King Edward VII. When introduced to the straight-laced king, the former popcorn salesman didn't bow. He didn't stand politely, waiting for the monarch to greet him. Instead, he pushed passed the royal attendants, shoved the gum into the king's hands, and exclaimed: "Your Majesty, I'd like you to have a box of my chewing gum. You've never tasted anything as refreshing. Here, try a piece, Ed . . ."

At one time, bobbies (English police officers) received orders from Scotland Yard forbidding them to chew gum while on duty. The reason? Gum might get stuck in the bobbies' whistles during an emergency!

King Edward was flabbergasted. No one had ever dared speak to him in such a brazen manner. But he managed to pull himself together and thank White for the gift. Then, mopping at his brow, he hurried from the room, calling off all audiences for the rest of the day. Although the king hadn't tried a piece of Yucatan, White wired back home that the monarch had chewed every stick and loved it. News services picked up the wire and printed White's boasting, and sales for Yucatan increased in the United States and England.

Despite William White's bad manners, by the end of World War I, chewing gum had spread throughout the British Isles. Although the habit was still looked upon as improper, one writer admitted it was at least " . . . a hundred times more natural than cigarette smoking or the use of lipstick . . ."

GAMU'S THE WORD

The Orient. Many people stereotyped the far east as the land of Buddha and Confucius, silk fans and samurai, tea, jade, and the spice trade.

But by the early 1900s, this ancient world was fast becoming an industrialized culture. Many of its people enjoyed the conveniences and pastimes of modern life but they had yet to experience chewing gum.

William Wrigley, Jr. decided to change all that.

In 1913, Wrigley set sail for the Orient, hoping to create a new market for his gum. First stop: India, where thousands of people enjoyed chewing betel nuts, the fruit from a native pepper plant. Wrigley hoped to convert these betel chewers to gum. But Wrigley's campaign failed, despite thousands of dollars spent on promotion and advertising.

A new organization called the Let's Chew More Gum Association opened an office in Tokyo in 1962. To celebrate, the Association threw a gigantic party, complete with movie stars, famous baseball players, popular politicians, and sumo wrestlers. The evening ended with a religious ceremony. A Shinto priest stood before an elaborate altar, chanting a prayer that praised the "Great Spirit of the Chewing Gum."

At first, Wrigley feared Japan might prove as gum-proof as India. Japanese journalists warned their readers that gum chewing led to other bad habits. Wads of ABC *gamu* (gum) were suspected as disease carriers. Government officials banned gum in several districts. To make matters worse, many people didn't understand that gum was only for chewing —and insisted on swallowing it.

To solve this problem, Wrigley hired university students and other honored members of the community

68

to give gum lectures. They traveled from village to village, accompanied by a brass band and banner-wielding peasants. Before a curious crowd, the lecturers would hold up a stick of gum, unwrap it, place it in their mouths, and chew . . . but not swallow. The gum was then properly thrown away.

To clean up gum's dirty image, Wrigley next developed a series of advertising campaigns in Japan's major cities. Billboards popped up all over Tokyo, the country's capital. Every carnival and fair featured a chewing gum booth. During baseball games, scoreboards explained what chewing gum was before listing the score.

If you're planning a trip to Singapore, don't take a pack of bubble gum with you—unless you want to be arrested. Government officials banned the manufacture, sale, and importation of chewing gum there in 1991. The reason? Too many people were throwing away chewed wads in public places, causing "filthiness." The final straw came when the doors of subway trains kept jamming because of the sticky stuff. Anyone caught importing a pack of gum is fined $6,250—or a year in jail!

Gamu's popularity increased. But Wrigley still faced a major problem. Most Japanese earned less than ten cents a day. To expect workers to spend half that amount on a pack of gum was unreasonable. So Wrigley allowed shopkeepers to open the packs and cut each stick in two. For one *sen* (about half a penny), a worker could buy half a stick of gum.

Later, Wrigley developed this same pricing system in China. According to *The Great American Chewing Gum Book*, ". . . not one Chinese in 10,000 could afford to buy a whole stick of gum." Wrigley solved this problem by giving shopkeepers a pair a scissors to cut each stick in half. A thrifty peasant could make his half stick of gum last anywhere from a week to almost a month.

But in China, Wrigley faced another problem. Most peasants were superstitious. They believed that any design (such as the drawing of a pack of gum) combined with the printed word (such as a billboard) was evil and represented demons. As a result, Wrigley's widely successful billboards could not be used. Instead, informational bulletins were produced and planted across the countryside. Each one explained what gum was and bore only a very small picture of the product.

Slowly, the peasants came to accept these bulletins and soon their fears disappeared

altogether. The trademark of another American gum company even resembled the outlines of Chinese architecture, as well as the characters of their written language. The peasants believed this to be a good omen and began chomping those demons away. By 1935, over a million dollars' worth of gum was selling in China every year.

This love of gum was short-lived, however. Two years later, when the Japanese Army invaded China, a rumor spread that chewing gum had been invented by the enemy. The

Chinese believed it. They became convinced that all gum brands, including Wrigley's, were manufactured in Japan. When the Chinese government banned the sale of Japanese goods, chewing gum was also boycotted. It would remain forbidden in that country until the end of World War II.

Bubble Gum? Just Say Nyet

The Berlin Wall crumbled in 1990, and for the first time since 1961, the people of Eastern Europe are enjoying new freedoms every day, including the freedom to chew gum. But forty years ago, chewing gum was illegal in all Communist countries. Many, like East Germany, considered gum a "symbol of American debasement of European culture."

But people chewed it, anyway—when they could find it.

In the 1950s, kids begged it from foreigners on the street. People wrote to friends and relatives living in the United States, asking for it. Gum smuggling became common, and a black market began, with individual sticks selling for thirty cents a piece. In Czechoslovakia, seven students were so desperate for gum that they produced their own brand called Breezy—which they made from candles. They secretly sold the gum for fourteen cents a stick. It sold well until the government discovered the underground factory and threw the students in jail.

But that didn't stop the smugglers. Gum was "flowing into the schools from unknown sources and by unknown roads," bemoaned one teacher. Nothing could be done.

Finally, in 1957, the Communist authorities gave in.

In Czechoslovakia, for example, the government opened a factory and immediately produced twenty tons of gum. At first, they sold it only to coal miners, hoping to break the miners' habit of chewing hunks of tar. But soon the gum was made available to everyone.

Poland followed suit, calling gum chewing "a perfectly harmless recreation."

Even East Germany allowed a synthetic rubber factory to produce chewing gum. They advertised it as well. A magazine ad featured a photograph of children pulling strings of gum from their mouths. The caption read, "An old and always new game that gladdens the heart of every child."

Unfortunately, the hearts of Russia's children remained sad. Authorities there refused to lift their gum ban. Patricia Nixon decided to break this gum barrier when she and her husband, Vice President Richard Nixon, visited the Soviet Union in 1959. Mrs. Nixon brought along a trunk filled with candy and gum to hand out to children who greeted her. The kids wolfed down the candy bars—but seemed afraid to touch the gum.

"My daughter loves it," Mrs. Nixon coaxed as she handed a pack to one young boy. "She chews and chews." She unwrapped a stick for him, but the boy burst into tears. Mrs. Nixon never found out if the boy was frightened because he'd never seen gum before . . . or if he knew he'd be punished if he chewed it. To save other children from fear and embarrassment, Mrs. Nixon put the gum back in the trunk. For the rest of her trip, she gave away only candy.

It would be seventeen years before the Soviet Union lifted its ban on gum. In 1976, the country produced 28,000 tons of its first batch of *zhevatelnaya rezink* (gum). Authorities boasted that the gum "cleans and strengthens the teeth and helps blood circulation in the mouth." But children didn't care how healthful the product was. They were just happy to say *da* to bubble gum.

3 . . . 2 . . . 1 . . . BLAST OFF!

Today, 550 gum companies in 93 countries produce chewing gum for people around the world. Turkey heads the list with 60 gum manufacturers. The United States is in second place, followed by England and then Canada.

You can find a chewing gum factory near the wondrous pyramids of Egypt. In South America, natives have replaced their habit of chewing raw chicle with "chingongo" (their pronunciation of chewing gum). You can buy Dubble Bubble in Spain by asking for "Dooblee Booblee." And Admiral Richard Byrd, an American explorer, took chewing

Chewing gum first went into orbit when astronauts Edward H. White II and James A. McDivitt smuggled the stuff onboard their space capsule during the *Gemini IV* mission in June 1965.

gum on his five expeditions to the South Pole, saying it helped calm his nerves.

Chewing gum has even been to outer space.

The *Gemini V* astronauts first officially took gum into space in 1965. (Each of their food packages contained a meal and two sticks of Trident sugarless gum.) But *unofficially*, gum boldly went where no gum had gone before a few months earlier. Astronauts Major James A. McDivett and Major Edward H. White II had smuggled the stuff on board their space capsule before blasting off on the *Gemini IV* mission. And a good thing, too, as Major McDivett explained: "At some point Ed's toothbrush got lost. We don't know whether it floated out of the spacecraft along with his glove when the hatch was open [during the space walk] or what. Anyway, I didn't try to brush my teeth, so they got a little furry. We had gum on board to freshen up our mouths."

And what did the astronauts do with their gum when they finished chewing it? "They swallowed it," a NASA spokesman claims. *Hmmm.* Is it possible the gum actually floated out of the spacecraft? Perhaps it still orbits the earth today . . . a true glob around the globe.

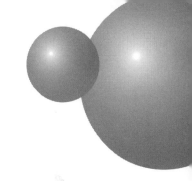

"I'VE GOT AN IDEA!"
WHERE NEW GUMS COME FROM

"This gum," Mr. Wonka went on, "is my latest, my greatest, my most fascinating invention! It's a chewing gum meal! . . . Just a strip of Wonka's magic chewing gum—and that's all you'll ever need at breakfast, lunch and supper! This piece of gum I've just made happens to be tomato soup, roast beef and blueberry pie . . . !"
—Willy Wonka in *Charlie and the Chocolate Factory*, by Roald Dahl, 1964

Decisions, decisions.

You walk into a store, plunk down your money, ready to buy a chewy chunk of bubble gum.

But how do you choose?

Do you want your gum gooey like toothpaste? Coiled like tape? Do you want it shaped like a pizza? A crayon? A bloodshot eyeball? A hot dog squirted with a "mustard" candy coating?

What about flavor? Something fruity, perhaps, such as watermelon, raspberry, blueberry, or grape? Or are you thirsty for some lemonade, root beer, or chocolate shake gum? How about a flavor so sour, your whole face puckers? Or so hot, your nose starts to run?

Bubble gum comes in a variety of shapes, flavors, and more. And although you can't yet buy the Wonka three-course-meal gum, you can bet that someone, somewhere is working on it.

Who are the Willy Wonkas of today? Who decides what your gum will look like, taste like, chew like? Where do they get their ideas? And how do they turn those ideas into something you can sink your teeth into?

HOME IS WHERE THE GUM IS

Tom Berquist sits at his kitchen table, surrounded by a group of neighborhood kids. He holds up a drawing. "What if the gum ball looked like this?" he asks. "Would you buy it? Chew it? Tell your friends about it?"

The kids answer at once, voices tumbling over one another. "Yeah! That looks good! I love it!" They laugh. Berquist smiles. He's just invented a bubble gum that could become next year's megahit.

Berquist is marketing director for Stanico, Inc., a small private company that makes non-chocolate candy products. His job is to come up with ideas for new candy and gums—not only what they'll taste like, but what they'll look like and what they'll be called. He's most famous for inventing Boogers, the candy kids love to hate.

Sound like fun? Berquist thinks so. But it's hard work, too. The idea is just the start. First comes what Berquist calls "the narrowing process." He breaks this down into four main questions.

1. **What will be the size and shape of this gum?** For example, Berquist might choose a chunk gum, stick gum, or a gum ball.

2. **Can we produce this size and shape in our factory?**

3. **Is there a place for this gum in the market?** Has someone already invented a gum like this? If so, Berquist may have to scrub his idea. Or he'll have to think of ways to make his product or packaging a little bit different.

4. **What are the fads of today?** The gum must either fit into one of those fads or it will have to start a new fad of its own.

Next comes "the creative process." Berquist, who lives across the street from a school, invites students over to help. The kids gather around his kitchen table while he brainstorms, tossing out ideas for gum names, flavors, colors, and packaging.

"I look for an emotional response from the kids," Berquist explains, "because the key is to 'tickle' the customer. To come up with an idea that's playful, fun. So if the kids laugh, or shout, 'Yeah! That's great!'—I know I'm on to something. If I get a ho-hum response, if they yawn and say, 'That's cute—then I chuck the idea.'"

Berquist works with groups of students ages eight to twelve, or twelve to fifteen. That's because kids in these age groups usually have their own money. They buy their own gum, whereas children younger than eight don't buy much candy on their own—their parents buy it for them. Also, Berquist says, adolescents can generally explain their thoughts and opinions more clearly than younger children.

After a brainstorming session, Berquist takes the successful ideas to the drawing board. He makes a full-color illustration of the product, complete with packaging and printing,

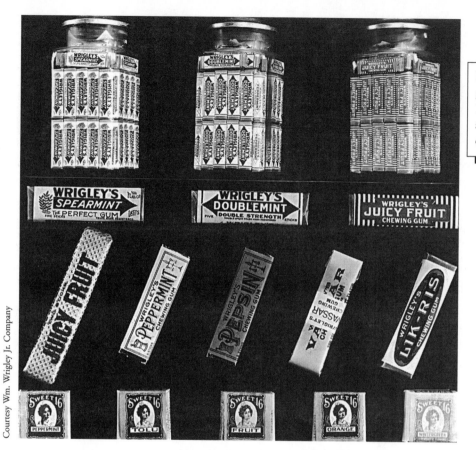

Packaging for gum in the 1890s was simple yet eye-catching.

and invites the kids back for a second look. "How about this?" he asks. "What do you like—or don't like? Do you like the name but not the package?" Again, Berquist looks for a strong emotional response. If the students are enthusiastic, he moves on to the development process.

At this stage, Stanico produces a prototype, or a sample, of the gum for the kids to try. "If you hate something, tell me you hate it," Berquists tells them. "I don't want you to be polite. I don't want you to answer the way you think you should answer." Then he hands

One hundred years later, in the 1990s, gum is packaged to look playful, fun, or funny.

Courtesy John Wardlaw

out gum, and the students start to chew.

Some gums bomb big-time. Take, for example, Frost Balls.

"I had created a sweet-minty gum ball with a frosted coating on the outside," Berquist says. "The coating had menthol in it that would evaporate as you chewed, giving your mouth a refreshing *whoosh*. Adults liked it. But the kids who tried it said, 'Yuck! It tastes like toothpaste!' or, 'Ew! It's mediciney.' We decided to try selling the gum, anyway. But after a few months, we pulled it off the market. Kids just wouldn't buy it."

Sometimes the fads of yesterday can be transformed into the fads of today. In 1979, Amurol Products, a subsidiary of the Wm. Wrigley Jr., Co., created Chew-Bops, bubble gum shaped like records. The company packaged the gum in reproductions of original album covers that had become collector's items among rock fans. As with most fads, the novelty of Chew-Bops eventually wore off—and Amurol was stuck with thousands of round bubble gum molds. Years later, they came up with an idea: Turn the recordplatters into pizzas. Today, you get five pink "slices" of Domino's Pizza brand bubble gum inside every box. And if you look carefully, you can find the hole from the record spindle hiding underneath each "pizza pie."

Other gums are an instant success. Berquist's test audience loved Oogly Eyes, gum balls that look like—you guessed it—eyeballs. Oogly Eyes has been popular for more than five years, a long time for a novelty gum, Berquist says. "Kids try Oogly Eyes the first and second time for the fun of chewing an 'eyeball.' But after the novelty wears off, they keep buying it again and again because of its good value. For only five cents, they get a large-sized chunk of gum that tastes great."

The kids in Berquist's neighborhood agree. Let's hope Tom Berquist continues brainstorming gummy ideas—with a little help from his friends!

How Much Is That Bubble In The Window?

Larger companies develop their ideas for new gum products in a more formal way.

Howard Granner, marketing manager for Leaf Canada, a company well-known for its Rain-blo Bubble Gum Balls, says: "Coming up with an idea is a team effort. Our marketing people start with a name or a concept. Then we brainstorm, working backwards. For example, we might say, 'Let's make a celebrity bubble gum.' Then we ask: 'What would celebrity gum look like? What exactly is it? What could it be?'

"Other times we might come up with a crazy name first and then see if an artist can create something visually on a box or package. The packaging is very important. It has to be an eye-catcher."

Sal Ferrara, president of Ferrara Pan Candy Company in Chicago, agrees. "When a kid goes to a candy counter," Ferrara says, "he has twenty-five or fifty cents. The candy counter is twenty to thirty feet long, and he can only afford to buy one or two items. The graphics must catch him."

"Kids vote for what they know," says Tom Berquist. "Young buyers want something that's familiar, yet new. So we have to create a product that looks like something they've tried before, yet better. More fun. That way, they'll want to chew it again and again. And they'll tell their friends about it, too."

That's why gum companies, big and small, get advice directly from their best customers: kids!

At Leaf Canada, Granner finds out what kids like—and hate—with the help of surveys compiled by a marketing-research company. The company polls kids ages eight to twelve to give their opinions of new bubble gums. This testing process is similar to Berquist's—except these kids receive twenty-five to thirty dollars an hour!

For the survey, panels of six to eight kids sit in a comfortable conference room. At one end of the room is a round table for the kids. At the other end is a one-way glass: the kids can't see out, but the survey-takers can see in.

One or two moderators will bounce ideas around or show the kids packet boards—posters with full-color drawings of new gum products. The kids are asked to give their honest opinions.

"If they don't like something, boom! We start over," says Granner. "A lot of ideas die on the vine. Kids thought our pancakes-and-syrup bubble gum sounded disgusting. The same with our peanut-butter-and-jelly gum. Once we came up with a great concept called Fire and Ice. The gum ball would taste hot on the outside and cool on the inside. We thought it'd be a hit. But the kids surveyed couldn't understand how a gum could be both flavors at the same time, and gave it a thumbs-down."

After Granner receives the survey results, he puts the gums that receive a thumbs-up into production. (It usually takes six months from the time of the concoction of an idea to the delivery of a new bubble gum into stores.) Then the whole process starts over again. Leaf develops about fifteen to twenty new candy products every year, including at least one new gum flavor every six months. Fads come and go quickly in this business, Granner confides, and competition is tough. So the surveys are very important in discovering which bubble gums will appeal to kids today—and tomorrow.

"DOES YOUR CHEWING GUM LOSE ITS FLAVOR ON THE BEDPOST OVERNIGHT?": QUALITY CONTROL, RESEARCH AND DEVELOPMENT

> *I could hear Teresa chomping her bubble gum. Grape today, so
> it must be Tuesday. Teresa chews a different flavor every day of the
> week. Banana on Monday, strawberry on Wednesday, root beer
> on Thursday, regular on Friday, cinnamon on Saturday.
> On Sundays, she chews all the flavors at once. Gross!*
> —Jeffrey, in *Me + Math = Headache,* by Lee Wardlaw, 1986

A sign on the laboratory door reads QUALITY CONTROL, RESEARCH AND DEVELOPMENT.

83

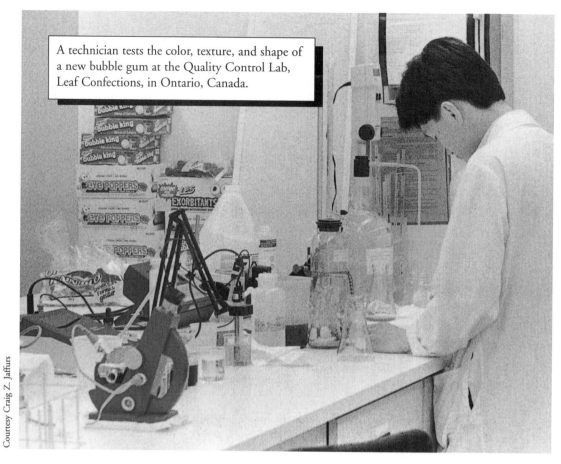

A technician tests the color, texture, and shape of a new bubble gum at the Quality Control Lab, Leaf Confections, in Ontario, Canada.

But what really goes on inside?

Will you find bubbling beakers, fizzing flasks?

Counters covered with coils and wires, zapping and crackling, and hissing kettles that spit and overflow?

Will a Dr. Frankenstein-like scientist shuffle through the hot steam toward you, holding a frothing test tube that smells like dirty socks—and pork chops? "*Ah, you're just in time to sample my new gum,*" he cackles. "*WOO-HOO-HA-HA-HA!*"

Hardly.

Yes, the chemists conduct experiments here. But the lab is air-cooled and spotless. Countertops are polished. Beakers gleam. The floor looks clean enough to eat off. It should be: This is where new gums are created, flavors are mixed, textures are tested. Every ingredient is inspected. This rigorous process guarantees that each piece you chew will *always* be good.

Flavor factories rarely use natural flavors for bubble gum. Instead, they mix chemicals to simulate natural flavors (four chemicals are mixed to create strawberry). This is because so much flavoring is needed. For example, to make enough strawberry-flavored gum for only one average-sized U.S. city, manufacturers would have to use America's entire annual strawberry crop!

STEP INTO MY PARLOR . . .

"Welcome," says Maha Reddy, manager of quality control at Leaf Canada. He wears a white lab coat and beckons toward his lab. "Allow me to show you what we do here."

He leads the way to a long shelf containing rows of small, dark-tinted bottles. Each bottle has a label: BANANA . . . PEACH . . . CHOCOLATE . . . PEANUT BUTTER . . . GRAPE . . .

"These are liquid flavors," Reddy explains. "After the marketing department comes up with a new idea for bubble gum, they turn the concept over to us. We make a few gum samples, experimenting with these flavors. Then we must ask ourselves three important questions:

"1. Does the gum taste good?

"2. Does the gum meet our high standards?

"3. Will this gum be cost-effective? Which means, can we afford to produce this gum and still make money for the company?

"If we can answer yes to all three questions, the company will give us a green light to produce the new gum."

Does Reddy himself invent the flavors? "Oh, no," he says. "All gum manufacturers buy them from flavor factories."

Also known as flavor houses, these are companies that produce millions of different flavors and fragrances, which are then used by a variety of manufacturers in foods, beverages, gum, and even shampoo. Bubble gum flavoring isn't just for bubble gum anymore. You may have tasted or smelled it in juice drinks, candy, surf wax, toothpaste, and lip gloss.

Chemists at the flavor factories work to brew and stew new flavors, as well as to improve old ones that have become fads in other foods.

Japanese chemists recently invented what they call Mood Gum. Like the Mood Rings popular in America in the 1970s, Mood Gum changes color when you're happy, sad, angry, etc. The change takes place when the acidity level in a person's saliva rises or falls.

"People say, 'I tasted something in ice cream and thought it would be good in candy,'" explains Chuck Rogers, vice president of operations at Bell Flavors and Fragrances.

The same goes for gum. For example, not long ago you may have raved about a bubble gum flavor called blue raspberry. To you, it was a new taste sensation. But blue raspberry had already been popular for years in Kool-Aid, Sno-Kones, and Popsicles. There are fashions in food, just as there are in clothing. And both go out of style quickly.

For example, citrus and other fruit flavors have been wildly popular the last few years. So have super-sour and super-hot gums. But by the time you read this, these gums might be ho-hum. What will be the next flavor fad? "If I could predict that," says Phil Sprovieri from the flavor company McCormick and Wild, "I wouldn't worry about winning the lottery!"

MMM-MMM, GUM!

After a flavor is chosen for a new bubble gum, a lot of work remains before the gum can go into production.

"First, we must decide the level of the flavor, or how strong the flavor will be," Reddy says.

"Next, we test the flavor for what's called the fall-off intensity. In other words, how long will the flavor last? Ideally, gum would have a great taste that lasts ten to fifteen minutes. But right now, most bubble gums keep their zip for only a minute or two—five at the most. That's because flavorings dissolve fast with saliva."

Reddy once taste-tested an experimental gum said to keep its flavor for *five hours.* "I can't say for sure the flavor lasted that long," admits Reddy, "because after chewing for one-and-a-half hours, my jaws got tired—and I threw the gum away."

A five-hour gum sounds great, but it might have one major drawback: price.

"The process to make long-lasting gum is expensive," Reddy says. "So we'd have to charge kids more money for the product."

Another problem concerns the complex ingredients needed. The U.S. Food and Drug Administration (FDA) considers gum a "food product." Because of this, all ingredients must meet strict standards.

Reddy says a plan for a glow-in-the-dark bubble gum was once discussed. But he had to scrap the idea because "some of the dyes needed might be unhealthful, and therefore wouldn't be approved by the FDA."

A flavor that *has* been approved is Buttered Popcorn.

Reddy points at the bottle sitting on his desk. "Go ahead," he urges. "Unscrew the cap and sniff. *Zing!* Smells just like hot-buttered popcorn, doesn't it? We plan to use it for popcorn-flavored gum balls.

"At first, our marketing people wanted the gum to *look* like popcorn. But popped kernels come in all shapes and sizes. It was too hard to get the same number of popcorn in each package. So now we hope to sell them in a movielike popcorn box."

Sergio Nacht, vice president of Research and Development at the Wm. Wrigley Jr. Company, has invented the first long-lasting gum using "micro-sponges." The tiny sponges are designed to trap flavors in the "nooks and crannies" of a wad of gum. Then, they release the flavor slowly each time the gum is "squeezed" or chewed.

TESTING: ONE, TWO, THREE . . .

If the popcorn gum balls are a success, is Reddy's work over? No, he insists. There's still much to do after the gum comes out of production.

"Before the gum balls are shipped," he says, "chemists, lab technicians, supervisors, and managers must all do random sampling. We taste-test the gum balls to make sure they have a good chew. The gum can't lie flat in your mouth. It must be soft enough to munch, but resilient enough so that it springs back again and again."

The key to good gum is consistency. Each gum ball must have the same weight, shape, color, and flavor.

To ensure this, quality-control labs check what is called the "shelf life" of a bubble gum. Often, gum will sit on a shelf in a store for five or six weeks before every piece is sold. It is Reddy's job to make sure the gum does not grow stale during that time, or lose its color, texture, or shape. So the lab is stocked with large jars of gum, each one labeled with the date the gum was produced.

"Here, try one," Reddy says, offering a two-month-old gum ball. Sure enough, it tastes and chews just like the one that is fresh off the production line.

Sometimes gum samples are also placed in incubators to see if any bacteria will grow. "No water is used in the gum mixtures," Reddy explains, "so growth is usually not a problem. The gum base and sugar are boiled at high temperatures, then cooled. Plus, sugar, glucose, and the syrups we use are sterile materials."

To flavor its famous Spearmint gum, the Wm. Wrigley Jr. Company grows enough mint every year on U.S. farms to fill 16,300 football fields!

Not so with chicle. Because of its great "spring-back," it's still used in high-quality gums—but only in small amounts. Chicle is difficult to clean and can easily become contaminated. But gone are the days when you might have found insects and twigs in your vat of chicle. Quality control experts see to that and more in gum companies all over the world.

SNAP, CRACKLE, POP!
HOW BUBBLE GUM BALLS
ARE MADE

Start with lots of silliness,
blend in pink balloons.
Stir until it bubbles
in a pot of afternoons.

Sprinkle in sweet lollipops,
a pinch of summer sun.
Fold in cups of chewiness,
then simmer till it's gum.
—*"Recipe for Bubble Gum,"* by Dian Curtis Regan

If you wanted to make bubble gum in the 1930s, you would have needed a large machete, a large kettle, and an elephant.

Make that a *large* elephant.

Back then, manufacturers made bubble gum from jelutong, a rubberlike latex found in the evergreen trees of Malaysia. A machete was used to make V-like cuts in the trees to allow the milky fluid to ooze down into buckets. After collecting the latex, workers boiled it in huge kettles over outdoor fires to form it into a thick mass, which was then poured into rectangular wooden molds. When cool, the heavy blocks of gum were hauled out of the jungle on the backs of elephants.

The best jelutong resin comes from mature evergreen trees at least thirty years old. When each tree is "milked" or "tapped," it yields only about two-and-a-half pounds of latex. Four or five years must pass before the tree produces enough resin to be tapped again. This makes the natural gum rare and expensive. That's why most manufacturers now use synthetic rubber or plastics for their bubble gum—materials similar to those used in golf ball covers.

Times change. Today, almost all manufacturers use imitation gums for their gum products. The blocks of gum now arrive at factories by truck or railroad car. Modern technology has made the production of bubble gum fast, efficient, and sanitary.

But even a little gum ball goes through a complex process before it can bubble and pop.

To make their bubble gum balls, Leaf uses 68,000 pounds of gum base, 100,000 pounds of dextrose (a type of sugar), and one quarter of a million pounds of powdered sugar per week.

FIVE STEPS TO SUCCESS

Mario D'Acri is processing supervisor at Leaf Canada, where the popular Rain-Blo Bubble Gum Balls are made. Today, D'Acri will be your tour guide. But before you can enter the manufacturing plant, you must take off any jewelry, put on a white lab coat, and tuck your hair into what looks like a shower cap.

Don't feel silly. All workers in the plant are dressed the same way. The company has strict rules and regulations about keeping the factory clean and sanitary. D'Acri says he doesn't want any stray hairs or earrings gumming up the works.

"Gum balls go through a five-step production process, which takes about three days from start to finish," D'Acri explains. He leads the way into a large room lined with rows of huge vats and kettles. Rectangular flats of hard gum base are stacked nearby. A sugary-sweet smell fills the air, tickling the back of your throat.

"Step one is called 'the forming process,'" D'Acri continues. "First, our workers break up the gum base into small pieces and heat it in these kettles.

"As the gum base heats, it melts, thickening like molasses or maple syrup. The syrup is then filtered

Bubble gum balls are made by slowly mixing gum base, sweeteners, and softeners together in giant vats.

to get rid of impurities and pumped into vats along with glucose, a sweetener. Glucose helps to keep the gum moist and easy to chew. Later, when we add powdered sugar, the glucose will also help it stick to the gum."

Each vat is equipped with giant blades that slowly revolve to mix the ingredients for about half an hour (Some vats can mix two thousand pounds at a time.) The gum now resembles bread dough the color of ash.

As the blades knead the gum, powdered sugar is added, followed by softeners, such as glycerin or other vegetable oils. Softeners keep the gum moist and flexible for a good, springy chew. Finally, natural or artificial flavoring is added.

All the while, the giant blades keep turning. Already, the bubble gum is living up to its name: The twisting and churning action of the mixers causes bubbles the size of basketballs to form and pop.

Next, D'Acri escorts you into a more spacious room. Conveyor belts crisscross above your head.

After the gum is blended, he explains, it is extruded or pushed through a machine, the same way toothpaste is squeezed from a tube. This forms it into a smooth, continuous rope, similar to the "snakes" you may have made by rolling clay back and forth between your hands. Pencil-thin snakes become

The Topps Chewing Gum Company makes their Bazooka bubble gum in a factory that is 400,000 square feet. That's the size of eight football fields, laid end to end.

regular-sized gum balls. Thicker snakes become gargantuan balls, like jawbreakers.

Whatever the size, the ropes of gum then travel along the conveyor belts into cooling tunnels, which surround the gum with cooled air to reduce its temperature.

The conveyor belts and tunnels look like an elaborate amusement park ride, a Disneyland for bubble gum.

"The forming process is almost complete," D'Acri says. "Remember—not a single human hand ever touches the gum. Everything is done automatically, by machine."

You watch as special blades cut the ropes into measured segments. The segments continue their ride into a rolling machine that spins and twirls them on a large corkscrewlike mechanism. The twirling action forms them into perfectly rounded balls.

"When I was a boy," D'Acri confesses with a smile, "I used to think each and every gum ball was formed by hand. If that were true, can you imagine how many workers we'd need? We make billions of bubble gum balls here every year!"

He plucks one off the conveyor belt and offers it to you. You shake your head. The gum is still an unappetizing gray color. You decide to wait and see what happens during the next step of production.

WOW . . . GROSS!

While in the rolling machine, the gum balls have heated up again. Now they must travel through another cooling tunnel. The tunnel rumbles like a mini-earthquake, shaking gently back and forth to keep the texture and shape of the balls uniform. Any that get flattened on one side are rejected and thrown away.

"This is the grossing process," states D'Acri. "The gum balls tumble through one last tunnel, and roll out into plastic crates. Workers stack these crates in our storage facility, which is climate-controlled. The temperature in there is about 64 degrees Fahrenheit. The gum will remain at that cool temperature for twenty-four hours, until the balls harden enough to coat."

The gum will also be tested by quality control technicians. These specialists inspect ingredients and conditions daily to make sure the gum is of the highest quality.

The Finishing Line

Your guide continues the tour. As you approach the next room, you hear a sound like rocks crashing down in an avalanche.

Curious, you cover your ears—the noise hurts!—and walk inside.

"This is the Finishing Room," D'Acri shouts over the din.

You glance around. Each long wall of the room is lined with giant potbellied kettles, their wide mouths gaping. The kettles are filled with gum balls in red, orange, blue, green, pink, yellow, and white. They rotate, tumbling the balls over and over like laundry in a clothes dryer. But unlike socks and T-shirts, these hard balls produce earsplitting sounds as they roll against each other. You watch for a few more minutes, breathing in the sweet fruity scent that surrounds you. Finally, the noise drives you back into the other room.

D'Acri chuckles as you massage your ears. "Our workers in the Finishing Room wear

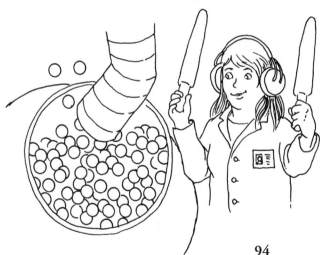

special headphones to block out the noise," he says. "They are similar to what ground crews wear at airports to protect their ears from the deafening jet roar."

But what exactly happens in the Finishing Room?

"After the grossing process," explains D'Acri, "workers scoop about three hundred pounds of balls into each of

During the forming process, gum is pushed through a machine the way toothpaste is squeezed from a tube. This forms the gum into smooth, continuous ropes.

Courtesy Craig Z. Jaffurs

Color and liquid flavoring are ladled into large kettles that can hold three hundred pounds of gum balls. The kettles rotate, tumbling the balls so that each one is coated evenly.

those tumbling kettles. Then powdered dextrose is ladled in, along with color and liquid flavoring. The tumbling action makes sure each gum ball is coated evenly. It also helps to remove moisture. This procedure takes about one hour and twenty minutes—including loading and unloading the kettles.

"When the finishing process is done, then we begin the glazing." D'Acri guides you toward the next room, which is just as noisy. "Once again, the gum balls are scooped into kettles and tumbled. When the final coat of liquid color is ladled in, the tumbling motion polishes the gum, which produces a glazed or glossy look. Beeswax is also added to give the gum extra shine."

The two of you move away from the din. You pass a long conveyor belt with rollers. "Some of our gum has writing or designs on it," D'Acri says. "That gum goes through our Branding Department. Each of these rollers is etched with printed words or an illustration. It picks up edible, quick-drying ink and rolls the design onto the balls as they pass under. If the gum has no design, then it goes directly from the Glazing Process to the final step: Packaging."

Bubble gum is 22–25 percent gum base, 12–20 percent corn syrup, 1–2 percent color and flavoring, and 50–60 percent sugar. There are about 20 calories in each piece of gum.

The Wm. Wrigley Jr. Company uses enough cardboard every year for packing its gum to cover a sidewalk 1,700 miles long. That's a cardboard sidewalk that would stretch from Chicago, Illinois, to Las Vegas, Nevada!

GOOD THINGS COME IN SMALL PACKAGES

The tour of Leaf's gum ball factory is coming to a close.

"The gum balls travel along this next set of conveyor belts into the packaging machine," D'Acri explains. "The machine automatically wraps the gum in plastic and seals it with heat." (Some gum-wrapping machines have up to 16,000 moving parts!) "Technicians oversee the process to make sure everything runs smoothly. Then they load the individually wrapped pieces of gum into boxes or plastic bags, which are sealed airtight and marked with a quality assurance date. The gum is then packed into shipping cases, and sent to hundreds of thousands of stores all over the world."

D'Acri motions you toward a stairway. "Come, let me show you something."

You follow him up the stairs. You find yourself on a catwalk, high above the factory.

You look down and suck in your breath.

Below stands crate after crate, brimming with a rainbow of gum balls, all glossy and glowing under the bright lights of the factory. The crates are stacked almost head-high, in rows that stretch as far as you can see.

"And that's just one-and-a-half days' worth of gum," D'Acri says.

You let out your breath in a low whistle.

Your guide leads you back downstairs, then out into the bright sunshine. You thank him for taking the time to show you around.

"You're welcome," he says, and hands you a large, sealed box. "Oh, and here's a little souvenir of your tour. Something to remember us by."

You wave and walk away. You don't open the box. You don't need to. Inside you know what you'll find: enough bubble gum balls to make any kid happy.

THIS LITTLE BUBBLE GOES TO MARKET:
DISTRIBUTION AND PROMOTION

"We bubble heads do not like to be mean, but we are desperate,"
says Regor with a giggle. "Our whole planet depends on
bubble gum. We must eat at least three packs a day to survive.
But our supply is running out. Your planet has plenty of gum.
Why, we hear that children on Earth chew gum just for fun
and then stick it on the bottoms of chairs and desks
when they get tired of it."
—from *The Amazing Bubble Gum Caper,*
by Jane O'Connor and Joyce Milton, 1983

A sunny Saturday afternoon. You're hanging out with your friends, having fun, feeling fine. When suddenly, *WHAM!* It hits you.

You recognize the symptoms: pink bubbles floating before your eyes . . . the urge to move your jaws up and down . . . the need to inflate someting soft and chewy . . .

The diagnosis is clear. You're having a *bubblemaniac attack.*

You don't need a doctor—you already know the cure. You need some bubble gum, and *fast*. But where can you go?

The answer is: everywhere (or just about!).

Supermarkets, restaurants, drugstores, and candy shops. Convenience stores, airports, railroad, bus, and subway stops. Gas stations, stadiums, theaters, and newsstands.

But how does bubble gum get to all these places?

It all begins back at the bubble gum factory.

THE BIG THREE

Three groups of people are responsible for supplying you with bubble gum.

The first of these is the **manufacturer.** As described in Chapters 9 and 11, the manufacturer comes up with new ideas for gum size, shape, and flavor. It produces the gum in its factories and then designs unique packaging for it.

The manufacturer sells and ships the finished product to a wholesaler. This is a company that buys the gum in large quantities at a very low price.

The wholesaler then sells and delivers the gum to the retailer—a store—that offers it at a higher price to the customer.

This sounds like a simple process. But sometimes, as Adams and Wrigley could attest, it isn't easy to convince wholesalers and retailers to take on a new product.

"There's a lot of competition—a lot of bubble gum—out there already," explains Tom Berquist from StaniCo, Inc. "Some of the manufacturing companies have been around for decades. And their bubble gums are proven sellers. So wholesalers and retailers think, 'Gee, why do we need another five-cent gum?' We must convince them that our gum is special. Different. Delicious. And prove that it has tested well with kids."

But what if the manufacturers don't?

"Then the retailers won't carry our gum in their stores," explains Berquist. "And kids will never have a chance to try it."

Crates filled with bubble gum balls wait to be packaged and shipped to wholesalers.

To increase their chances with retailers, manufacturers introduce new products with the help of sales reps. While they no longer hawk their wares from a horse-drawn wagon like Wrigley and Adams did, the rest of the process is much the same.

The sales reps bring samples. While the wholesalers chomp and chew the new gum, the reps give a sales pitch about why their gum would appeal to kids. They emphasize its packaging and demonstrate the types of eye-catching gum displays, including counter bins, freestanding shelves, and special dispensers that attach to cash registers.

Sales reps also attend trade shows or conventions, such as the Candy Exposition sponsored by the American Wholesale Marketers Association (AWMA). At least twice a year, over one thousand candy, gum, and snack food manufacturers from all over the world attend these shows to exhibit their goods.

Launching a new gum product is chancy and expensive, so these sales reps must be very good at their jobs. They must know everything about their product and show they believe it can be a success. In the long run, this salesmanship is what will convince the wholesaler to give the new gum a try.

After the wholesalers choose which gums they wish to carry, they place an order. The sales reps forward the order to the manufacturer's warehouse, which ships the gum out immediately by truck to the wholesaler's warehouse. In some cases, the gum is shipped directly to a store's main branch. This store will send the gum to other outlets in its chain.

NEXT!

Once the wholesalers have bought a new product, it's up to their own sales reps to convince the retailers. Grocery stores, delicatessens, mom-and-pop shops, and other small outlets are all targets in this next round of sales pitches. Sales reps also make sure orders are filled for gum ball machines.

To entice retailers into buying more gum, the sales reps often offer premiums—just as Wrigley did 100 years ago. The retailer may keep the premiums or give them away as promotional items. Coupons and free samples nudge buyers into trying the new product.

Sales reps check back with the retailers again and again to make sure they're satisfied with the gum. Companies such as Amurol Products (a subsidiary of the Wrigley Company) review their national retail customers at least twice a year to find out what's hot and what's not at certain locations. If a gum isn't working, they try to replace it with one that will. Sales reps try very hard to keep their customers happy. If they don't, they could lose important refill orders.

THE ROYAL RETAILER

Manufacturers may design the materials and programs to boost gum sales. But in the end, the retailers are king. They're the people who put the gum in front of the customer.

Retailers do this most often by creating catchy displays near the cash register or check-out counter. That's because gum is an "impulse item"—something people buy on the spur of the moment.

Imagine: You're in a long, boring grocery store line with your mom. As you wait for her to pay, you notice a large display of gum. Looks good, you think. The next thing you know, you're pulling on your mom's sleeve, begging: "Please may I have a pack of gum? Please, please, puh-lease?" Chances are, she'll let you. That's an impulse buy: Neither you nor your mom planned to buy the gum until you saw it in front of you.

Retailers aim to give as much space to candy and gum as possible, expecially in high-traffic areas. "If you bury [goodies] near laundry detergent," say Ross Colletti, a marketing consultant who worked for American Chicle for thirty-three years, "then you're not going to sell as much because not everybody buys laundry detergent." That's why the checkout counter is such an ideal spot.

DOUBLE YOUR PLEASURE, DOUBLE YOUR FUN

Just about everyone knows the Wrigley's Doublemint jingle. You hear it on TV. You hear it on the radio. When you see that famous green wrapper, you even hear it in your head. Wrigley's "tell 'em quick and tell 'em often" advertising campaigns have helped make his gum popular worldwide.

So why don't you hear jingles or see ads for *your* favorite chewing gum?

"Large, well-known companies don't need to advertise," says Tom Berquist, "because their products already have name recognition. And small companies can't afford to advertise. Radio, TV, and newspaper ads are very expensive."

As a result, many manufacturers use other schemes to promote their products.

"The key is to be innovative," says Berquist, "to create a gum that looks so fun, you don't need to advertise it beyond displaying it in the stores." That's why many gums have wacky packaging, such as toothpastelike tubes or pizza boxes, or seasonal packaging where bags of gum are decorated with Halloween, Christmas, or other holiday pictures. That's also why some gums come with a novelty or toy. The combination costs more, but you can still play with the toy after you've chewed the gum.

"Packaging and toys are expensive to produce," says Howard Granner of Leaf Canada, "so we specialize in unique flavors and displays. For example, we make big baskets to sit on cash register counters, which are filled with our Peach Sundae, Apple Cinnamon, and other fruit-flavored gums."

"June and July are bad months to promote gum," says Granner, "because the kids aren't around. They're usually at camp or on vacation."

"Back-to-school months like August and September are especially good," he continues. "A lot of students stop off at convenience stores such as 7-Eleven to buy goodies on their way home from school. And our attention-grabbing promotions are on display, to let kids know what new gums we've created for them."

Some companies sponsor nationwide promotions. Nabisco hosts the Super Bubble Yum Blow-Out every year. In this contest, kids aged six to fourteen compete to see who can blow the biggest bubble. Winners receive savings bonds to use toward college, as well as computers, video games, VCRs, and cases of bubble gum. The contest provides the company with good publicity and helps kids pursue their college dreams.

The Wm. Wrigley Jr. Company says there is probably "no other product available to the consumer in so many different locations as chewing gum." Bubble gum is tasty and comes at a low price. Because it's so popular, most stores keep plenty on hand. So the next time you feel a bubblemaniac attack coming on, relax. You're sure to find some bubble gum right around the corner.

GOODNESS, GRACIOUS, GREAT BALLS OF GUM: GUM BALL MACHINES

"You can set your gum ball machine down in the most unlikely place—say, the middle of the Sahara [desert]— and someone, possibly a camel, will come along and play it."
—from *The Trouble with Gum Balls,* by James Nelson, 1956

The instructions are simple:
Drop in a penny. Crank the dial. Take out the gum ball. Pop it in your mouth. Chew.

Gum ball machines are easy as A-B-C. So easy, you'd think Americans would be bored with them by now.

Not a chance. Gumball machines are here to stay. People today find them just as fascinating and fun as our great-grandparents did 100 years ago.

Snort, Cluck, and Chomp

Historians claim that vending machines date back as far as the first century A.D. None of these machines has survived to the present day. But a few from eighteenth-century England can give us an idea of what they were like.

In the 1700s, vending machines were called Honor Boxes and could be unlocked only with a coin. Some supplied tobacco and snuff. Others were more elaborate, such as the Bull's Head. If you put in a penny and pulled down on one of his "horns," he would snort a douse of perfume onto your handkerchief. Another Honor Box looked like a chicken. Insert a dime, and with a cluck-cluck-cluck she laid you a hard-boiled egg!

Over a century later, in the 1880s, Frank H. Fleer, inventor of Chiclets, would be one of the original manufacturers to sell gum from a penny vending machine. But he took some coaxing. When a salesman first asked him to buy a few of the machines, Fleer said no.

The salesman refused to take no for an answer. He insisted that people found the machines so fascinating, they'd drop pennies in them for nothing. Fleer took the bet and agreed to buy several of the salesman's machines if the boast came true.

The salesman chose his site: the entrance to the Flatiron Building in New York City. One reason why tourists often visited the building was because of the odd gusts of wind that whirled around it. The salesman set up his vending machine—illegally—with a sign bearing these instructions: DROP A PENNY IN THE SLOT AND LISTEN TO THE WIND BLOW. Hundreds of people did. Before the hundreds could turn to thousands, however, the police hauled away the mechanism.

Fleer was convinced and immediately ordered his first vending machines.

In the late 1880s, Thomas Adams, inventor of the original chicle chewing gum, created the first vending machine for gum balls. He filled his machines with Tutti-Frutti, his fruit-flavored gum balls, and set the vendors along the elevated-train platforms of New York City. Travelers loved the convenience, and the machines were an instant success.

FORD HAS A BETTER IDEA

Despite their popularity, early gum ball machines did have a few problems. Some arose when kids jammed buttons, fake coins, and chewed wads of gum into the coin slots. Poor design caused other problems. Since the machines were not airtight, the gum got stale or wet, causing the glossy colors to run and fade.

Not much could be done about the kids. But a Baptist minister solved the design problem.

A roofing salesman named Ford Mason leased 102 gum ball machines in 1918, hoping to start a new business. He filled the machines and set them up in a variety of stores in New York City. They did not do well. The machines were so unreliable and the gum of such poor quality that people rarely returned to buy more.

Mason's father, a Baptist preacher, heard of his son's troubles. To help him out, he set about creating a modern, dependable gum ball dispenser. (The machine is so dependable, the same basic design is still in use today.) He patented the mechanism and then turned it over to his son to produce. He also encouraged the young man to start his own gum-manufacturing business.

Mason agreed. He named his new venture the Ford Gum & Machine Company, hoping people would connect him with Henry Ford, the famous car manufacturer. Then he convinced shopowners across the country to set up the new machines in their stores. The merchants would receive 20 percent of the earnings.

This giant gum ball machine in an Oklahoma City mall holds up to nine thousand gum balls the size of tangerines.

The earnings were big. Mason's black, red, white, yellow, pink, green, and orange gum balls were a hit—especially since he worked constantly to improve their texture and flavor. During the next ten years, he also experimented with a special glazed coating that could make the gum balls water-repellent.

"In the old days," Mason said, "a drop of water would ruin the colors of a barrel of gum balls. Of course the gum still tasted good, but nobody wanted gum balls that looked stretched and spotty."

Mason didn't have to worry anymore: His experiments succeeded. "You [could] take a handful of treated gum balls," he said, "and hold them under a running faucet without any color coming off."

Over the years, the Ford Gum & Machine Company expanded to produce both sugarless and aspirin gums, which people chewed to ease a sore throat. Mason also helped to create a branding machine that marked the gum with his logo at an astonishing rate of 250,000 gum balls per hour.

In 1939, Ford initiated the program he's most famous for: "Chew for Charity."

A hospital in Columbus, Ohio, desperately needed money for medical equipment in its children's ward. A women's club asked local store owners if they would donate their 20 percent commission from Mason's gum ball machines to the hospital. They agreed. Six months later the club had enough pennies to buy everything they needed to complete the children's ward.

The success of the "Chew for Charity" program impressed Mason so much that he developed the Fordway Program.

Mason Ford retired from the gum ball business in 1970, but still enjoys talking about the early days of gum. He especially likes to tell one story about a psychology professor who taught at Syracuse University in New York. The professor wanted to see how and if monkeys react to different colors. He trained a number of laboratory monkeys to insert pennies into the slots of Ford's machines and then remove the gum balls. His studies showed the monkeys reacted the same as most kids: They "sulked" when a white gum ball popped out, and "jumped with glee" when they received a colored one.

Today, six thousand charities and community clubs sponsor his gum ball machines in stores across the country; 20 percent of the company's annual profits—about 200 million pennies—are donated to these organizations every year.

How Charm-ing!

Gum balls aren't the only things you find in gum ball machines. Drop in fifty cents and you also get a prize.

Lyle Becker has been in the gum ball machine business for over fifty years. His company holds the honor of being the first to combine gum and toys in a single machine—thanks to peanuts!

Becker's father owned a cigarette vending-machine business and dabbled with candy and peanut machines on the side. He sold the business to his son in the late 1930s when the boy was in high school. Becker and three of his buddies studied the business and realized the food machines made more money. They dumped the cigarettes, and L. M. Becker & Company was born.

Unfortunately, the boys discovered that peanuts and candy bars went stale fast in the machines. Sales dropped. So, back to the drawing board.

That's when Becker hit on the idea of selling gum balls.

"The bubble gum balls worked great," said Becker. "Before we knew it, we had three hundred machines in various outlets all over the Midwest." Then Becker added a few striped Winter Balls to the usual rainbow-colored gum as a promotional gimmick. Any kid lucky enough to get a striped gum ball would receive a five-cent candy bar from the shopowner. Sales increased.

Then the United States entered World War II. Before long, sugar and gum shortages forced Becker to go back to selling peanuts. But this time he filled his machines with small charms to add some appeal.

"Everything was in short supply in the 1940s," Becker said. "We could sell anything for a penny—even peanuts! But people really loved the charms." When the war ended, Becker returned to selling bubble gum balls—but continued his new sales gimmick.

The charms came in all shapes and sizes. Since war was still on people's minds, a military series was a big success. It included charms that looked like guns, tanks, army jeeps, walkie-talkies, and grenades. A Wild West series featured cowboys, boots, buffaloes, stagecoaches, horseshoes, tomahawks, and tepees. Charms also came shaped like hearts, pencils, snakes, propellers, razors, and even the Statue of Liberty.

Becker's business continued to grow. Soon, the one-cent gum vendors were set up in over five thousand locations from Connecticut to Nebraska. The future looked great—until the Health Department stepped in.

"They were afraid the charms might contaminate the bubble gum," Becker explained. "We were really worried for a while. If the Health Deparment shut us down, we would've lost everything! Fortunately, they later reversed their ruling, and we were allowed to continue the business."

Then, in 1950, another problem cropped up. The state of Wisconsin, where Becker's company was based, declared the machines a form of gambling. That's because each machine held only one charm for every three gum balls. Every time you dropped in a penny, you took a chance; there was no guarantee you'd receive both gum *and* a prize.

Again, Becker worried he'd be shut down. But when the front page of a major newspaper ran a story about the "gambling" problem, Becker's machines sold out instantly. And the furor blew over.

As years passed, the prizes became more popular than the gum balls. So Becker added more elaborate toys to the vending machines: miniature decks of cards, knives and harmonicas, stone rings from Czechoslovakia, tattoos, rocket ships, even fake false

Trivia question: In the early 1950s, what future U.S. president did Ford Company hire as its radio gum ball spokesman?

Answer: Ronald Reagan

teeth! At first, Becker's company made most of the charms, but eventually they bought them in Hong Kong, where the goodies could be produced at a lower price.

For the last twenty-five years, Becker's company has manufactured Toy 'n' Joy Centers: vending consoles as large as video games or soda machines. Each unit has several smaller vending machines within it. Some sell gum balls the size of tangerines. Others sell plastic digital watches, troll dolls, plastic insects, or chicken eggs with a surprise inside. The high-tech centers are in most grocery stores. But the standard gum ball machines with the fire-engine red base and upside-down fishbowl are still around, too, in bowling alleys, pizza parlors, family restaurants, roller rinks, ice-cream parlors, and candy stores.

Some modern gum ball vendors are as large as video games or soda machines.

112

BASEBALL AND BAZOOKA JOE:
BUBBLE GUM CARDS
AND COMICS

Basketball can be a thrill!
Hockey takes a lot of skill!
Football players work real hard,
And baseball players pose for cards.
All the games are tons of fun,
But nothing beats my bubble gum!
—rap from a Bazooka Joe comic

Bazooka Joe is wrong.

Yes, bubblemaniacs spend $500 million a year on bubble gum.

But a promotional gimmick created to help sell more gum now racks up annual sales of *$75 billion.*

The gimmick?

Bubble gum cards.

Take Me Out To The Ball Game

The original bubble gum cards didn't come with any gum at all. In the 1870s, cigarette manufacturers hoped to increase sales by inserting picture cards into packages of their products.

The gimmick worked. People enjoyed collecting the cards, which featured photos of flags, famous ships, Civil War generals, and Indian chiefs. Card collecting became so popular that candy, cereal, and even bread companies started offering cards in their packages.

Baseball cards stepped up to the plate next. The first ones appeared in a pack of Old Judge cigarettes in 1886. The photos were printed on sepia-tone paper and hand-colored with expensive dyes. The players were photographed in a studio, so some of them looked pop-eyed from the burst of flash powder. Others looked stiff and uncomfortable, probably because they were posed to hit a baseball suspended from a string.

Few of these early cards exist today, but the ones that do are worth a fortune. The most valuable card of all is of Honus Wagner, considered by the Baseball Hall of Fame to be the "greatest shortstop in baseball history."

In 1909, Wagner discovered that the 20th Century Tobacco Company had used his photo without permission on a card in packs of their cigarettes. A nonsmoker, the ballplayer hated the idea of kids taking up the habit. He threatened to sue, and the company agreed to remove the card from circulation. Unfortunately, sixty of the packs had already sold, and could not be recalled. Eleven of Wagner's cards survive today: In 1996, one sold for half a million dollars! For that reason, the Honus Wagner 1909 T206 is considered "the King of Baseball Cards."

An upscale mail-order catalog recently offered a gigantic gum ball machine. It stands five feet six inches tall, and holds nine thousand oversized gum balls. The machine sells for $1,995.00—plus $175.00 for shipping it to your home.

During World War I, the entire card-collecting industry shut down. Paper and printing presses were needed for the war effort, not for "frivolous" gimmicks.

After the war, former collectors were slow to renew their interest in the cards. But the invention of bubble gum in

1928 sparked new life into them. The Goudney Company of Boston, National Chicle of Cambridge, and the Bowman Chewing Gum Company all introduced cards with their bubble gum in the 1930s. Sales soared, and "bubble gum cards" became a household phrase.

Unfortunately, World War II was just around the corner. From 1941–45, materials used in the production of gum and cards were needed desperately for the war. Most companies hung in as long as they could. Topps Chewing Gum, Inc. even created a successful "plane spotters" card series for civil defense. But shortages eventually caused the bubble gum card industry to close down once more.

Topp That!

After the war ended another kind of battle began: the Battle of the Bubble Gum Cards.

By 1948, rationing was over. Companies rushed to offer the gum-and-card packages again. Each wanted to outdo the other and gain control of the market.

Bowman launched a baseball series with forty-eight black-and-white cards.

The Leaf Company of Chicago retaliated with the first set of color cards.

Then Topps fired off a set called Magic Photos. These featured bubble gum cards of movie stars, war heroes, test pilots, basketball players, and even dogs.

After a brief retreat, Bowman fought back the following year. He managed to sign most of the big-league ballplayers to exclusive contracts. This meant the players could not pose for any company except his own. With his new set of 240 cards, all in color, he blasted his competition out of the water.

Bowman had won the battle. But he had yet to win the war.

Two years later, in 1951, Topps put eleven Hall of Famers under contract. They posed for a card set called the Connie Mack All-Stars, named after the manager of the Philadelphia A's. That same year, Topps released its first series, made up of two individual sets of fifty-two cards each. Demand was high—each set of cards could be used to play a tabletop game of baseball.

The Goudney Company of Boston, Massachusetts, was the first to release a series of baseball cards with bubble gum. Several kids noticed that number 106 of this 1933 set was missing and wrote to the company to complain. This posed a problem: Goudney had never made number 106. The following season, the company printed a small special order of number 106 cards and sent one to each child who had written. No one noticed that the ballplayer was Napoleon Lajoie, who hadn't played baseball since 1916.

Topps topped itself the next year with the largest set to date: 407 cards. These extra-large cards featured color photos of ballplayers on the front. The flip side highlighted team emblems, game stats, and personal information about the players—the first cards to do so.

For the next few years, Topps and Bowman continued their fight for control of the bubble gum card market. But in 1955, Topps signed almost all of the major baseball stars for its cards. Bowman had to admit defeat. The next year, he surrendered and sold out to Topps—which remained on top for more than two decades. By 1976, the company had sold a quarter of a billion cards and two hundred tons of bubble gum!

THE GREAT TRADE OFF

Baseball cards have been the most popular of all cards for most of this century. But other topics have proved hot sellers. A Davy Crockett series available in the early 1960s (the same time the Davy Crockett TV show aired) sold 300 million packs. Fans also loved cards featuring Elvis Presley and the Beatles.

But it was the Wacky Packs series produced by Topps in the 1970s that broke all sales records. Wacky Packs cards made fun of well-known products. Takeoffs on brand names included Sneer Laundry Detergent, Peter Pain Peanut Butter, and NeverReady Batteries. To handle the long lines of young buyers, some stores in New York City opened separate cash registers exclusively for sales of Wacky Packs. Fleer's Dubble Bubble soon joined the act with its Crazy Cover series, making fun of magazines with names such as *U.S. Booze and World Report, Slime,* and *Newsleak.*

Today, Topps still has the exclusive right to sell card-and-bubble gum combinations. But a 1981 court ruled that anyone can make picture cards—as long as they aren't sold with gum. These are now called trading cards.

Most of the trading cards available today are produced and sold by a few major companies, including Topps, Fleer, Score, Upper Deck, Pro Set, and Impel. Half of all trading cards sold are baseball cards, but that proportion is shrinking slowly. You can now buy cards featuring TV and movie stars, famous authors, sports figures, dinosaurs, operas, musicians, foreign countries, and political figures. As part of a recent antidrug campaign, the U.S. Customs Service issued a set of cards celebrating their team of dogs.

Trading-card collectors can find these and other cards in grocery, specialty, and convenience stores. They read hundreds of books on the subject and attend conventions to buy, sell, trade, display, or play their cards. The only thing they *can't* do is expect to find bubble gum in the card packages—unless they're part of a series called Topps Kids. This set features 132 cards made especially for kids just starting the trading-card hobby. It also includes cartoons, trivia, and of course, a stick of bubble gum.

BAZOOKA JOE AND HIS GANG

The gimmicks don't stop at bubble gum cards. Manufacturers also use a trick that tempts you toward bubble gum and tickles your funny bone at the same time: comic strips.

Bubble gum comics were created to distinguish the different brands after so many competitors had entered the gum business, says Walter Diemer, inventor of the first bubble gum.

The first comic insert came in packages of Dubble Bubble Gum, produced by the Fleer Company. With its heroes Pud and his friend Rocky Roller, the comic became an enormous success.

But even Pud and Rocky were no match for what would become the most famous gum character of all: Bazooka Joe.

Topps Chewing Gum, Inc., began producing Bazooka bubble gum in 1947. The gum first sold in five-cent chunks about the size of Tootsie Rolls. Some people believe Topps named its new bubble gum after the rocket-launching bazooka gun developed during World War II. But in fact, the name came from the popular U.S. comedian and entertainer Bob Burns. His 1930s radio act featured an unplayable musical instrument, which he made from two gas pipes and a whiskey funnel. He called it a "bazooka."

To help increase sales, Topps decided to offer smaller, one-cent pieces of Bazooka gum with a comic insert in each wrapper. A team of cartoonists were hired to create a strip, and in 1953, "Bazooka Joe and his Gang" made its debut. The strip starred Bazooka Joe, a blond kid wearing a red T-shirt, blue baseball cap, and a black eye patch. "We never explained what was wrong with Joe," says a Topps spokesman. "The eye patch was just added to make him distinctive."

The Gang included Mortimer, Joe's best friend, who wore a turtleneck sweater that covered most of his face; Herman, a chubby kid; Pesty, Joe's little brother; Jane, another friend of Joe's; Wilbur, a smart kid with glasses; and Walkie-Talkie, Joe's dog. Joe's white-haired "Ma" also appeared in the strip.

At the bottom of each comic you would find your Bazooka Fortune. *You have a good*

Bazooka Joe in 1955 . . .

head for figures, and will prosper if you enter the banking or accounting field, reads one fortune from 1955. Another one from 1957 says: *You are naturally artistic, but too much of a dreamer. Hard work will make your dreams come true.*

Kids who collected Bazooka Joe comics redeemed them for a variety of prizes. Save 100 comics and you could get two free adventure-mystery books. Or send in 125 comics, and you'd receive a necklace, advertised as a "swell gift for your girl." Other "free gift" ads featured baseball gloves, bracelets, harmonicas, sunglasses, ballpoint pens, magic tricks, binoculars, and key rings.

BAZOOKA JOE GETS RAD

From the 1950s to 1990, cartoonists drew between five hundred and seven hundred Bazooka Joe comic strips. (They were rotated every five to seven years to keep the jokes fresh.) But then Joe's popularity began to slide. Topps did some research to find out why.

. . . and Bazooka Joe in the '90s.

In late 1990, Topps interviewed numerous kids ages six to twelve in the New York area, as well as a number of adults. Everyone was asked how they felt about the comics, what they liked and didn't like.

The results? Most adults still loved the old Bazooka Joe strips. But the kids said they wanted characters who were more "hip."

Topps listened. Joe and his friends were transformed into modern teenagers with cool clothes, longer hair, and up-to-the-minute interests. New characters were also added: MetalDude, a heavy metal freak; Zena, Joe's girlfriend, whose motto is, "I'm Zena! I'm hot! And I love to shop!"; and Ursula, a physical-fitness fanatic. The characters now appear in four cartoon series called "Bazooka Joe Raps"; "Bazooka Joe & Company"; "Bazooka Joe Mystic Master of Space & Time"; and "Bazooka Joe Fantasies."

Topps has also updated the Bazooka Fortunes, abandoning the wise and serious advice of yesteryear for silly "messages with an edge." *Let nature take its course and hope it passes,* reads one comic. *You can count on others, but it's better to use your own fingers and toes,* states another.

Jefferson R. Burdick, of Syracuse, New York, holds the record for the largest bubble gum card collection. When he donated his cards to the Metropolitan Museum of Art in 1963, he had collected 200,000 cards—dating from the 1880s to the 1950s. The collection filled more than 100 scrapbooks.

The new and improved Joe has become a hit. And so has his bubble gum. Billions of pieces of Bazooka are sold every year in over thirty countries around the world. The comics appear in English, French, German, Spanish, Dutch, Hebrew, and Chinese. New flavors, including raspberry, cherry, appleberry, and strawberry, have also hit the market.

But the original Bazooka flavor remains the most popular. Topps seems to have taken its own advice from a recent Bazooka Joe comic:

Be yourself. It's who you do best.

CHAPTER 15

How to Blow a Bodacious Bubble: Advice from the Pros

*. . . once a day, a bubble pops
and people stop to stare
as the champion gum-bubbler
pulls the goo out of his hair.*

*Even with the sticky stuff
deflated on his face
he never gets enough of
blowing bubbles into space.*

*Even when the gum has lost
its spring, he won't relent.
He jaws it up and down until
it's tough as old cement.*

*Then he grabs another chunk
and starts to chew it silly.
That's why he's called the Bubble King,
our Bodacious Billy!*

—from "Bodacious Billy the Bubble King," by Ellen A. Kelley

The real-life King of Bodacious Bubbles is actually . . . a girl.

Susan Montgomery Williams, of Fresno, California, has reigned as official Bubble Queen since 1985. Her World Record bubble measured twenty-two inches—a whopper that remains undefeated to this day.

How did she do it?

Miss Williams isn't telling.

But the national finalists in a recent "Super Bubble Yum Blow-Out Contest" held in Chicago agreed to share the secrets of their success. The nine bodacious bubblers are:

Steven Schleder, age 14, from Virginia Beach, Virginia.
His first-place bubble measured 9 5/8 inches.

Jon Goerge, age 14, from Lansing, Michigan. His bubble placed second at 9 inches.

Anthony Getto, age 13, from Mesquite, Texas.
Anthony placed third with an 8 3/4-inch bubble.

Phillip Russ, age 14, from Fort Walton Beach, Florida.
Fourth-place bubble: 8 1/2 inches.

Ryshema Davis, age 12, from Orangeburg, South
Carolina. Fifth-place bubble: 8 1/4 inches.

Shandia Johnson, age 14, from Holts Summit, Missouri.
Sixth-place bubble: 8 inches.

Katie Thompson, age 13, from Colorado Springs, Colorado.
Her seventh-place bubble: 7 3/4 inches.

Mike Lugo, age 13, from Eau Claire, Wisconsin.
Eighth place: 7 3/4 inches.

Chelsea Corman, age 14, from Merced, California. Close
behind Mike with a bubble measuring 7 5/8 inches.

Nine national finalists in the 1992 Super Bubble-Yum Blow-Out Contest proudly display their trophies.

BUBBLEMANIA: How old were you when you first started chewing bubble gum and blowing bubbles?

CHELSEA: Five or six. I loved blowing bubbles because it annoyed my mom!

MIKE: Three or four.

SHANDIA: I was so young, I was crawling around picking gum up off the floor!

123

BUBBLEMANIA: How did you train for the bubble-blowing competition?

JON: The Bubble Yum people sent all the finalists a case of gum two months before the final contest. I chewed through the whole case—that's four hundred packs of bubble gum! I spent between twenty-five and fifty hours practicing.

ANTHONY: I practiced for about twenty minutes every day for five months.

CHELSEA: I trained by timing myself. The contest rules say you have five minutes to chew the gum, then two minutes to blow a bubble. So I would concentrate on getting the gum at just the right place in my mouth before blowing. And I would do it in under two minutes.

Edward L. Fenimore, who heads the Philadelphia Chewing Gum Company (which makes Swell Bubble Gum), is said to have blown a triple whammy: a bubble within a bubble within a bubble!

BUBBLEMANIA: How did your parents or friends help you to train?

RYSHEMA: My mother supplied all the gum.

STEVE: Everyone at school was supportive. But they were really surprised that I could win so much just blowing bubbles! (Steve won a $10,000 savings bond to use for education, plus a trip for four to Walt Disney World. He also won the first annual Super Blow-Out contest. For both victories, Steve won a total of $35,000 in cash and prizes.)

JON: My baseball team really helped. I'd hand out free gum at practice, and we'd have mini-competitions.

PHILLIP: My friends kept saying, "You can do it!" Some of them made fun of me, though. Others didn't believe that the contest was for real.

CHELSEA: My best friend cheered me on. She made the practicing fun. One time, I blew the biggest bubble ever—and it burst in her hair! We sat there for hours, picking it out. She was really freaking out, afraid we'd have to cut it!

BUBBLEMANIA: What did you like best about the competitions?

RYSHEMA: Blowing the bubbles!

ANTHONY: Getting to go to a White Sox game. (Bubble Yum paid to take all the finalists to a game.)

STEVE: The free stuff we got—all for blowing one little bubble!

SHANDIA: I liked being "famous" at school. The teachers asked me to blow bubbles in the school talent show. I didn't think I'd do very well, because they didn't give me the right kind of gum. But I blew a grape bubble as big as your head! Everyone was impressed.

CHELSEA: I loved getting to ride in a limo!

The first person to win the Chomp Queen title was Sue Jordan, who chewed eighty pieces of Doublemint gum for five hours and twelve minutes—or 15,600 chomps! Clyde Steward McGehee, of North Carolina, broke that record by chewing 105 sticks of Juicy Fruit gum for six hours. He finally stopped when he got hungry. Richard Walker, a Boy Scout, set the all-time chomping record: chewing 135 sticks of gum for eight hours.

New York teenagers Randi Grossack and Barbara Malkin hold the world record for weaving the longest gum wrapper chain: 196 feet, 8 inches. That's equal to 2/3 of a football field! Grossack and Malkin used 4,720 wrappers.

BUBBLEMANIA: What did you like *least* about the competitions?

KATIE: Sometimes there were sarcastic and rude remarks from people in the audience.

PHILLIP: The fear that I would have to go first! Also, the suspense. The waiting.

CHELSEA: I felt bad for the kids who didn't win.

SHANDIA: I got a little sick to my stomach. There were three rounds of competition, and we chewed three chunks of gum at once in each round. That's a lot of sugar!

BUBBLEMANIA: What is your secret for blowing a bodaciously big bubble?

MIKE: None of your business!

RHYSHEMA: I've been asked that question a million times, and I still don't know the answer. My secret is . . . just blow!

CHELSEA: You should try to get all the sugar out. Chew the gum for a full five minutes before blowing a bubble. And keep the gum dry.

ANTHONY: No, I don't think you should chew all the sugar out. It stretches too fast if there's no sugar left—and it'll snap or break. You don't want the gum slurpy, but having a little sugar left helps the bubble keep its shape.

PHILLIP: First, I roll up the gum in my hands into a big ball. Then I chew as much of the sugar out as I can. If you chew fast, you can do it in five minutes. Then, just concentrate on blowing a big bubble.

KATIE: Definitely practice a lot! For me, it just comes naturally, but I also work hard.

SHANDIA: Play the trombone! I've played for years, and that's helped to strengthen my lip muscles and control my breathing.

Relief pitchers Steve Olin and Kevin Wickander won the ESPN Great American Chew-Off in 1992. Both baseball players chewed seventy-one pieces of bubble gum at once for the required four minutes. "We are professionals," joked Olin. "Don't try this at home."

BUBBLEMANIA: Do you have any other words of bubble advice for the readers?

MIKE: Don't worry about blowing *big* bubbles. Just enjoy chewing gum and blowing bubbles with your friends.

CHELSEA: Never give up.

SHANDIA: Pucker up and blow!

STEVE: Have fun. That's the most important reason to blow bubbles!

Phillip Russ V blows a double-bubble during the National Competition of a recent Super Bubble Yum Blow-Out Contest.

Further suggestions for blowing big bubbles:

- *Flatten the gum on the roof of your mouth, or between your tongue and your teeth. Part your teeth a bit, then breathe out s-l-o-w-l-y until a bubble forms.*

- *Chew at least five sticks or five chunks of bubble gum, combined with a teaspoon of peanut butter.*

- *Chew the gum for a minimum of five minutes to dissolve most of the sugar.*

- *Experiment with different brands. Extra-soft bubble gum tends to work best for some bubblers; others prefer a stiffer chew.*

- *Will Tanner, a finalist in the First Annual Super Bubble Yum Blow-Out Contest, says: "It helps to have your two front teeth!"*

Renata Galasso Fordham worked her way through college in the 1970s by selling bubble gum cards. Fordham bought 10,000 packages of bubble gum, which contained a total of 13,000 cards. She arranged the cards into special sets, selling each one for $8.95. And the bubble gum? She gave it away to the kids in her neighborhood.

Topps holds the world record for having made the largest single piece of bubble gum. This gum was equal to 10,000 normal-sized pieces of Bazooka. Topps presented the gum to baseball player Willie Mays in 1974. Mays chopped it into smaller chunks and gave it away to children in nearby hospitals.

CHAPTER
16

THE MYSTERY OF BUBBLE GUM ALLEY

For better or ill
I sat on a stump
and was stuck by a lump
of gum on my rump
and am sitting there still.

—"For Better or Ill," by Julia Cunningham

N o one knows exactly how it started. Or when. Or why.

But one thing is certain: For more than thirty years, the origins of Bubble Gum Alley have remained a mystery. . . .

129

WALL OF WADS

Nestled halfway between San Francisco and Los Angeles lies the central coast town of San Luis Obispo (population 42,000). Every year, students from elementary schools throughout California take educational field trips to the town. Sometimes they visit the famous Mission, built in 1772. They tour the Historical Museum, or take a drive through Cal Poly (California Polytechnic State University). A picnic at Montana de Oro State Park is also a favorite.

But no matter where they go, they *always* find time to walk and gawk along Bubble Gum Alley.

At first glance, it looks like any other small alley: about six feet wide with two-story brick walls on both sides. Cool and partially shaded, it makes a nice shortcut to a parking lot.

Then, you notice the smell.

A faint sticky, sugary smell.

You do a double take.

That's when you notice the brick walls are coated with thousands of pastel-colored pebbles.

You peer closer.

No, not pebbles. Layers and layers of—ugh!—*chewed bubble gum.*

A STICKY PROBLEM

"We suspect Cal Poly students started the gummy tradition more than thirty years ago," says Mark Hall-Patton, director of the San Luis Obispo County Historical Society. "In the early 1960s, a few globs appeared on the walls. Then more. And more. By the 1970s, shop owners were complaining. 'The Alley is disgusting,' they said. 'Unsanitary. A blight on downtown.' They demanded the city clean and disinfect the area. But it was too late."

Thousands of ABC gum wads pebble the walls of Bubble Gum Alley, San Luis Obispo, California.

Courtesy John Wardlaw

By then, the sticky walls had become a tourist attraction. Reporters wrote articles about it. TV crews filmed it for Johnny Carson's *Tonight* show, *That's Incredible*, *Real People*, and PBS. Dozens of community members wrote letters to the editor of the local newspaper. They *liked* the Alley, they said. They wanted the bubble gum "mural" preserved.

Their support worked. The Alley was saved.

Meanwhile, gummers grew more creative. Instead of just tacking up a wad or two, they drew stringy pictures of lips, hearts, happy faces, and even cartoon characters. They created gum graffiti, spelling out their names and writing phrases such as "Sam Loves Shelby," and "Go Raiders!" Later, pencils, comics, pennies, glitter, Barbie doll heads, record albums, and yes, even bubble gum bubbles, were imbedded into the goo.

As the ground-level brick disappeared behind all this gum art, the gummers grew more daring. They brought out ladders in the dead of night, climbing more than fifteen feet to find a clean spot for their globby graffiti.

And Cal Poly students got into the act.

During its Week of Welcome (better known as WOW), the university organizes new students into teams of fifteen for orientation. Each team spends the first week at school together, learning about the campus and participating in activities.

"It's a tradition for the WOW groups to make themselves known at the Alley by writing out their team number—in bubble gum," says Cal Poly alum Kimberly Jensen. "I remember feeling dizzy, swaying toward the sticky, smelly walls. I wondered, too, if the Alley was getting narrower as the gum built up. Maybe someday it will be so small that only one person will be able to walk through it at a time!"

Rally For The Alley

By the mid-1980s, some residents and merchants had begun to complain again. "The Alley smells," they said. "It's disease-ridden. And ugly."

A cleanup campaign was discussed. But at the last moment, the community rallied to the Alley's defense. They popped off letters to the editor. They argued at city council meetings.

And with the help of these gum patriots, the Great Wall of Gum was saved once again.

Gumming Into The '90s

Today, Bubble Gum Alley is thicker and stickier than ever—in some spots up to ten wads deep.

"Yuck!" adults says. "Ewww! Ick! Gross!" A few hurry past, stop, and come back. "Is that what I think it is?" they murmur in wonder. "It *is!* Wow!" Others shake their heads, their noses wrinkled in disgust. Now and then, someone will glance around to make sure no one is looking, and then smack a huge glob of ABC gum on the wall before scurrying away.

And what do younger residents of San Luis Obispo think of Bubble Gum Alley?

"I think Bubble Gum Alley is a fun thing for kids to see, although I have never put a piece of bubble gum on the wall. I went to the Alley with my mom and brother. My brother and I had bubble gum in our mouths and wanted to stick them on the wall. But Mom said it was too dirty and disgusting, and it was a health hazard."
—**Alana Hein**, age 10

"I think Bubble Gum Alley is very cool. It's a great place to study bacteria. We should have the President [of the United States] put gum on it."
—**Logan Lossing**, age 10

"I think Bubble Gum Alley is an important landmark. It shouldn't be harmed in any way. It shows the messy side of San Luis Obispo."
—**Dana Aleshire**, age 9

"I like Bubble Gum Alley because I can put bubble gum on the wall and not get in trouble!"

—**Matthew Maier**, age 11

"I think Gum Alley is very fun and a nice place to visit. One time, though, I touched a piece of gum and it was wet. YUCK!!!"

—**Ann Marie Carlson**, age 10

What do *you* think of Bubble Gum Alley? Perhaps one day you'll get a chance to visit San Luis Obispo to see and smell the gummy, globby, gooey wall for yourself.

To find Bubble Gum Alley, take U.S. 101 freeway to San Luis Obispo, California. Exit at Marsh Street and head east. After passing Archer Street, go five blocks. Turn left on Chorro Street. Go one block. Turn left on Higuera Street. You'll find Bubble Gum Alley on your left, between 733 and 737 Higuera (right across the street from Tom's Toys).

Americans chew 90,000 tons of gum every year. That equals 180 million pounds of chewed wads. Imagine if all those wads found their way to Bubble Gum Alley!

RULES TO CHEW BY

Remove from mouth and stretch into a spaghetti-like strand.
Swing like a lasso. Put back in mouth. Pulling out one
end and gripping the other end between teeth, have your gum
meet your friend's gum and press them together.
Think that you have just done something really disgusting.

—"How to Chew Gum," from *How to Eat Like a Child*, by Delia Ephron, 1977

"**C**hewing gum . . . if it is done quietly and unobtrusively, is not unattractive," wrote Emily Post, the queen of manners. "But when one does it with grimaces, open mouth, smacks, crackles, and pops, and worst of all with bubbles, it is in the worst of taste."

Miss Post might sound old-fashioned. After all, you say, what good is bubble gum if you can't chomp, snap, *thwack*, crack, slurp, burp, and pop it?

Good point. Doing all these things is part of what makes bubble gum *fun*.

The problem is, it may not be so much fun for the people around you.

135

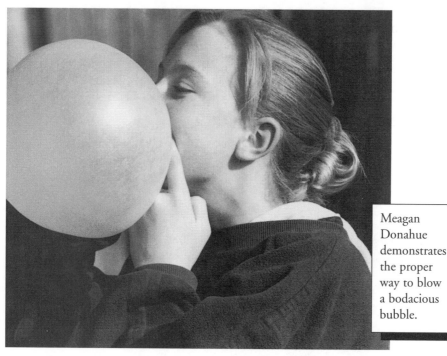

Meagan Donahue demonstrates the proper way to blow a bodacious bubble.

To keep gum chewing fun for everyone, sixth-grade students from Peabody Charter School, in Santa Barbara, California, gave the following advice:

- Always chew bubble gum with your mouth closed.
- Always give a piece to your friends.
- Always have gum in your pocket in case of an emergency.

—Beth Swihart

- Always hide your bubble gum on the roof of your mouth when a teacher is coming.

—Rudy Garcia

In the Czech Republic, gum chewing is called zvykacka—which translates to cud chewing!

- Stick your gum in the freezer when you're finished with it. The taste comes back!
- Never eat bubble gum off the ground.
- Never blow a bubble so big that it will pop on your face.
- Never eat gum older than you.
    —**Justin Matelson**

- Never put gum on a chair, because you'll get stuck.
    —**Elvira Flores López**

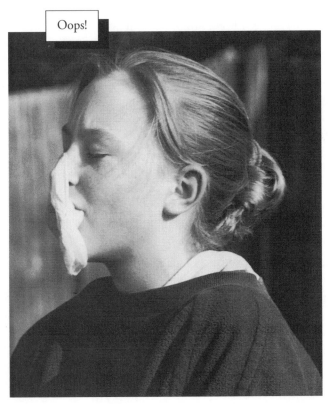

Oops!

- When speaking to someone, push the gum to one side of your cheek and stop all chewing motions.
- Never spit or blow bubble gum into the wind. (Results may be hazardous.)
    —**Seth Tufvesson**

- Never chew bubble gum too much, or else even when you aren't chewing, your mouth will keep going.
    —**Jordan Miles**

•Never chew bubble gum on a roller coaster, because when the roller coaster jerks, you might choke.
    •Never put bubble gum under a desk or chair, or in your sibling's hair.
    •Never give bubble gum to your dog. He might get better at blowing bubbles than you.
      —Amber Saucedo

•Always wrap chewed bubble gum in a piece of paper and throw it in the trash.
    —Humberto Gastelum

•Never blow bubbles in your friend's face.
•Never chew bubble gum when you have braces.
•Never chew bubble gum when you're sleeping, because it'll get stuck in your hair.
    —Kyle Erickson

•Always bring bubble gum on boats to repair leaks or holes.
•Never chew bubble gum in a pool.
    —Gary W. Johns, Jr.

•Always chew bubble gum until all the flavor is gone.
    —Sarah Teton

•Never smack your bubble gum in class.
    —Shannon Wagner

•Never use bubble gum as ear plugs or nose plugs.
•If you lose a tooth, always use bubble gum in its place.
    —Arturo Arellano, Jr.

•Never chew with your mouth open, because if you do, you will sound like a cow chewing grass.
    —Naomi Tipton

CHAPTER 18

BUBBLE BLOOPERS AND BLUNDERS
(AND HOW TO FIX THEM)

You stepped on some gum, it is true.
Don't worry, I know what to do.
Just go freeze the shoe,
then scrape off the goo.
Who cares if your foot freezes too?
—"Sticky Limerick," by Lisa Merkl

Admit it. You're a bubblemaniac.

You *like* being stuck on gum.

What you *don't* like is gum stuck on *you.*

No problem. At least not in the future. Someday, manufacturers will produce a bubble gum that's "ecology-friendly." According to Gary Schuetz, vice-president of marketing for Amurol Products, the gum will simply " . . . break down in your mouth." No muss. No fuss.

139

But until then, removing those gooey wads remains a sticky problem. If you make a bubble blooper or blunder, here are a few fix-it tips:

*To remove bubble gum from clothes or furniture:
Rub an ice cube over the chewed wad. This will freeze the gum, making it brittle. Gently chip or scrape away the frozen gum, using a table knife. (*Never* use a sharp knife!) If the piece of clothing or fabric is small enough, put the entire item in the freezer for ten to fifteen minutes, then chip the gum away.

*To remove bubble gum from the bottom of a shoe:
Try the ice cube trick. If this doesn't work, soak a cotton ball with rubbing alcohol or nail polish remover, and hold it against the wad for a few minutes. As with ice, this will make the gum brittle enough to chip away. Never use rubbing alcohol or fingernail polish on fabrics, except as a last resort. These products may damage the fabric or cause the colors to fade.

*To remove a bubble gum stain from fabric:
Have an adult use a grease solvent on the stain. If this doesn't work, take the material to a dry cleaner.

*To remove bubble gum from your body:
Take the remaining wad of chewed gum from your mouth and dab it against the strands stuck to your body (it comes right off). Wash with soap and water to remove the sticky feeling.

*To remove bubble gum from your hair:
Try rubbing a little peanut butter on the wad. The oils in the peanut butter may soften the gum enough to pull the goo off with your fingers. If this doesn't work, get out the scissors. You'll have to cut off the chunk of gum.

*To remove bubble gum from school benches, walls, floors, etc.:
For a single wad here and there, try ice. Bigger gum-graffiti jobs should be left up to the school custodian.

School custodians often use steam cleaners, chemical solvents, high-pressure hoses, and special scrapers to remove the globs. That can be expensive: One middle school in Glendale, California, recently spent almost three thousand dollars steam-cleaning the gum from its campus quad. A spokesman for the Los Angeles School District says that each of their fifty-four-person maintenance crew spends at least a half-hour every day scraping up gum.

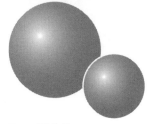

RECIPE FOR CHEWING GUM
A Home or School Project
(To be made with adult supervision only!)
Materials Needed:

Clean table
Cutting board
Rolling pin
Waxed paper or aluminum foil
Old wooden spoon (or a heavy-duty
  plastic spoon)
1 cup boiling water
1 teacup or coffee mug
Scissors
Small knife
Microwave oven or stove

Note: The chicle gum base is very sticky when it melts, which is why the Gum Kit contains a special plastic pan to use when you heat it. Do NOT use one of your own pans–you will find it very difficult to remove the chicle gum base afterward.

1 "Make Your Own Chewing Gum Kit" **
  which includes the following ingredients:
1 package chicle gum base (the stuff that
  looks like gray pellets)

1 pouch confectioner's sugar

1 pouch of corn syrup

2 flavor packets (peppermint and tutti-frutti)
1 black plastic pan (for microwave or stovetop)

**You may order a Gum Kit by sending $10 plus $2.50 for shipping (checks or money orders, no cash) to: VERVE, inc.305 Dudley Street, Providence, RI 02907. Telephone: 401-351-6415 Fax: 401-272-1204. Refills (gum base and special pan) are available for $6.00 plus $2.50 for shipping. Schools or organizations may order the gum base in bulk for special large group activities. Call VERVE, inc. for prices and shipping information.

Step One: Wash your hands.

Step Two: Stand the pouch of corn syrup in a teacup and pour in enough of the boiling water so that the water level is about the same level as that of the corn syrup. When the syrup is hot, it will be easier to pour out of the pouch.

Step Three: Sprinkle about half of the confectioner's sugar onto the table in a small mound.

Step Four: Remove the transparent cover from the black plastic pan and throw it away. Cut

open the plastic bag of chicle and pour the gum base pellets into the pan. Melt the chicle gum base, either in a microwave or in a pot on your stove top using the following instructions. (Remember: Do not use the transparent plastic cover. It will melt.)

If you're using a stove: Fill a 2-quart pot with about 3 inches of water, and place the pan in the water so that it is floating like a little boat. Cover the pot and boil the water until the chicle gum base is entirely melted. (This can take as long as 20 minutes.) Remove the pan.

141

**If you're using a microwave: BE CAREFUL—
even though the pan is made for microwaving,
it may melt if it gets too hot, so make sure to
remove it as soon as the chicle gum base is
gooey.** Since all microwaves are different, we
suggest setting the timer initially to 100%
power for 1 1/2 minutes. Then stir the gum
base to see if it is soft enough to work with. If
it isn't, put it back in for 30 seconds at a time,
then stir to see if it's done. When the gum base
has melted, it will look a little like flat, con-
gealed worms.

Step Five: Using the scissors, cut one end of the
corn syrup pouch and squeeze the corn syrup
into the chicle gum base. (Be careful—the
plastic pouch may still be hot from the boiling
water, so watch your fingers.) Stir the mixture
with the wooden or plastic spoon and empty it
onto the sugar mound on the table. (The gum
will be *very* sticky at this point.)

Step Six: Using your hands, knead the gum base
like bread dough. This means you will roll,
fold, tug, press, and squeeze the gum to make
sure the corn syrup, sugar, and gum are blended
well.

Step Seven: Using your fingers, divide the gum
into two parts on the table. Add the contents of
the tutti frutti flavor packet to one part, and the
contents of the peppermint packet to the other
part.

Step Eight: Mix the remaining sugar into both

parts. Continue to knead the gum base.

Step Nine: Roll out the gum, just as you would
cookie dough, until it is about 1/8 to 1/4 inches
thick. You may use a rolling pin, of course, or
even a can or bottle. Just make sure it's clean,
and sprinkle a bit of the sugar on it so that the
gum won't stick to it. (Or you can put a piece
of waxed paper over the top of the gum base to
keep it from sticking.)

Step Ten: Using the knife, cut the gum into
whatever size pieces you wish and chew a piece
or two (or ten!). The gum color will be a pow-
dery gray.

Step Eleven: Wrap up the remaining gum in
aluminum foil or waxed paper so you can save
some for later.

Step Twelve: Clean up. If by chance you get
some chicle gum base someplace it doesn't
belong, don't panic. Try dissolving it in melted
butter (not margarine) or using a commercial
solvent.

Author's note: It took me about an hour, from set-up to cleanup, to make this recipe. To melt the gum base in my
microwave, I heated it for a total of eight minutes on High. I
used a heavy-duty, plastic spoon to stir the gum, and threw it
away when I was finished. (The sticky gum base did not wash
off.) When the recipe called for kneading the gum base, I did
so for about five minutes each time to make sure the syrup,
sugar, and flavorings were well blended. If your hands get
tired, let family members, friends, or classmates take turns
kneading the gum. Instead of cutting all my gum into sticks, I
rolled about half of it into gum balls. (There's enough base to
make about 50 pieces or balls.) To protect your table, make

sure you place the gum on a cutting board before slicing it. The gum easily washed off the cutting board, rolling pin, and table with soap and warm water. If you have any problems removing the gum, and using melted butter doesn't work, please see Chapter 18: Bubble Bloopers and Blunders (And How to Fix Them) for more advice.

If you would like your gum to be a particular color, you can experiment by blending food coloring paste with the gum base and heated corn syrup. Or try adding 1 teaspoon glycerine and several drops of liquid food coloring. (For example, if you mix 6 drops of yellow food coloring with 3 drops of red food coloring, you will get orange-colored gum.) Food coloring paste is found at most bakery or gourmet specialty shops. You can buy glycerine at most drugstores.

To add color *and* different flavors to your gum, you can use any fruit-flavored powdered gelatin (such as JELL-O brand gelatin) or a small package of Kool-Aid soft drink mix instead of the peppermint and tutti-frutti flavors.

Happy Chewing!

After you've finished making the gum, here are a few other activities you can try:

1. Make up a name for your gum.

2. Design an eye-catching poster to advertise and promote it.

3. Create a newspaper or magazine ad. Don't forget a catchy slogan.

4. Write a gum commercial and perform it for your class. (Do this alone or with a group of friends.) If you have access to a video camera, film your commercial.

5. Write and sing a gum jingle.

6. Hold a bubble-blowing contest. Make up your own rules, deciding how many pieces of gum may be chewed at the same time, how much time each contestant has to blow a bubble, how long the bubble must last, how the bubble will be measured, who will judge the contest, etc.

7. Take several brands of store-bought gum to school. Hold a gum chewing test: Which brand tastes the best? Which flavor lasts the longest? Which is the easiest to chew? How does your homemade gum compare to the store-bought gum?

8. Design your own bubble gum cards. Cards could feature drawings of your heros, friends, teachers, pets, family members—even your favorite authors! Don't forget catchy slogans on the cards or important statistics on the back. (For example: Author cards could have pro-reading slogans such as "Get Stuck on Reading" or "Reading Is Wads of Fun." You could also list the names of the author's books, the prizes they've won, etc.)

9. Have your class sponsor a Bubble Gum Cleanup Day. Kids who scrape up the most chewed wads at your school could win a prize. Or, design special award certificates for the King and Queen of Gum.

10. Take a survey at your school. Ask kids such questions as: What can you do with chewed bubble gum? How do you blow a big bubble? What is your favorite flavor, and why? Publish the results of the survey in your school newspaper.

For Further Reading

Hendrickson, Robert. *The Great American Chewing Gum Book.* New York: Stein & Day, Publishers/Scarborough House, 1980.

Nelson, James. *The Trouble with Gumballs.* New York: Simon and Schuster, 1956.

O'Connor, Jane and Joyce Milton. *The Amazing Bubble Gum Caper.* New York: Scholastic, Inc., 1983.

Peeples, H. I. *Bubble Gum: Where Does it Come From?* Chicago, New York: Contemporary Books, Inc., 1989.

Plaut, David. *Start Collecting Baseball Cards.* Philadelphia: Running Press, 1989.

Poploff, Michelle. *Busy O'Brien and the Great Bubble Gum Blowout.* New York: Walker and Company, 1990.

Young, Robert. *The Chewing Gum Book.* Minneapolis: Dillon Press, 1989.

Acknowledgments

I would like to offer my thanks to the following people who assisted with the creation of this book. Thank you, one and all, for sticking by me—without you, I might've blown it!

Danny Arciero, Director of Operations, Leaf Canada Inc.; Lyle and Dolores Becker; Rebecca Berner, Director of Communications, San Luis Obispo Chamber of Commerce; Tom Berquist, Marketing Director, StaniCo Inc.; Timm Boyle, Senior Account Executive, Lesnik Public Relations; Hope Slaughter Bryant; Chuck Casto, Hunter MacKenzie, Inc.; Nicole Clemens; Chelsea Corman; Julia (Judy) Cunningham; Mario D'Acri, Processing Supervisor, Leaf Confections Ltd.; Ryshema Davis; Meagan Donahue; Roger Earls and his sixth-grade students at Peabody Charter School, Santa Barbara, CA; Alden Ford; Anthony Getto; Jon Goerge; Allison Gottwalt; Howard Granner, Marketing Manager, Leaf Canada; Mark P. Hall-Patton, Director, San Luis Obispo County Historical Society and Museum; Judith Herold; Sandra B. Horner, Coordinator, Media Relations, Warner-Lambert Company; Craig Jaffurs; Kimberly Jensen and her fourth grade students at Teach School, San Luis Obispo, CA.; Lyndon B. Johnson Space Center; Shandia Johnson; Ruth Katcher, my editor at Simon & Schuster; Brenna Kean; Ellen A. Kelley; Ginger Knowlton; Mike Lugo; Marni McGee; John McGrail Photography, Inc.; Lisa Merkl; Flontina Miller, Assistant Manager— Communications, Planters LifeSavers Divisions, Nabisco Foods Group; Stacie C. Moor, Administrative Assistant, Confection Marketing, Fleer Corporation; National Aeronautics and Space Administration; National Association of Chewing Gum Manufacturers; Maha Reddy, Manager of Quality Control, Research and Development, Leaf Canada Inc.; Dian Curtis Regan; Phillip Russ V; Steve Schleder; Sherry Shahan; Grace Siebert; Andriele Strodden; Clark Thomas, Associate Product Manager, Leaf Canada Inc., Illinois; Topps Chewing Gum, Inc.; Tricia Waddell; John Wardlaw, photographer; Barbara C. Zibell, Consumer Affairs Administrator, Wm. Wrigley Jr. Company.

Extra-special thanks go to Greg Barratt, President, Leaf Canada Inc., for arranging my visit to the Confection Convention, the tour of the Scarborough, Ontario, Canada, bubble gum "factory," and for all the free samples!

About the Author

Lee Wardlaw is the author of seveteen books for young readers, including *101 Ways to Bug Your Parents* (an *American Bookseller* 'Pick of the Lists') and *Seventh-Grade Weirdo* (a Florida Sunshine State Young Reader's Award book). Lee became a champion bubble blower at the age of seven, and spent many school hours secretly chomping, thwacking, and popping gum behind her math book. A former elementary school teacher, Lee now writes full-time from her home in Santa Barbara, California, which she shares with her husband, son, two cats, and an old-fashioned gumball machine.